The Chancer

HARPER & BROTHERS, PUBLISHERS, NEW YORK

THE CHANCER

BY MARSHALL PUGH

For Nanette

1

"I've got a feeling we're going to drift on like this forever," my wife said. "I'm bored with this, so bored."

We had been peaceful enough in April. We had spent our weekends in Sussex, walking in the woods which were dazed with spring, the young black poplars shivering in their sudden suits of light leaves, the azalea buds scented and ready to burst. But spring was passing, the last of the cherry blossom was blowzy, we were rowing again.

"Feel like going out tonight?" I asked.

"Do you feel like it?" she replied. I'd have liked to see a film, much better than to go with Helen to a pub where we would sit watching people, avoiding the eyes of the other watchers of people in the Chelsea Embankment pubs. But I'd already checked the cinema program and wondered why it was that the best floating releases in London always seemed to be washed up in Stoke Newington.

"It doesn't matter either way," I said, looking from the kitchen window into the yard of Sidney Court which faced north, on the site of the old brewery, between Albert Bridge and the first houses of Albert Bridge Road, on the Battersea side of the Thames.

A party of our neighbors was piling into a car to hurry across the bridge to the Chelsea side of the river, something they often did. They looked on Sidney Court as the cantonment for Battersea. It was cheaper to live on the unfashionable side of the river but they shopped in Chelsea, they drank in Chelsea, they had their clothes pressed in the King's Road, Chelsea. They sent their small children to nursery, pre-prep or even council schools in Chelsea and this was the traditional touch of cantonment life, for Chelsea was the Old Country—Home. There were a few inverted snobs in the Court who said that their flats were "in Battersea, between the Power Station and the Dogs' Home," but it was more usual for residents to say that they lived in "South Chelsea," unaware of lifting a revue line.

And we were suffering from the complaint that they had, "the Sidney Court complaint," brought on by the belief that life was being really lived somewhere else if only we could find it, probably just across the river on the Chelsea side.

"You decide, then," Helen said. "I don't care." She was folding something; she seemed often to be folding something, to occupy her hands. In one of her folding moods, she had trouble putting shoes away; she handled them several times as if she wished they had retractable heels. So I boiled a kettle and reached for the tin which normally held the tea. The tin was filled with brown sugar, the word *Beans* had been scored through and it now read *Split Peas*. I took the kettle from the boil and left it with the gas still burning. "I wouldn't waste gas if I were you," Helen said. "The garage bill's in the living room."

2

From the price charged for the radiator repairs, I could only assume that they had filled the radiator with heavy water. Then, when I was putting the bill away out of sight, I saw the Belgian doll. Helen had followed me to the living room. "Where did the doll come from?" I asked. "The Stephenses? Back from holiday? Wonderful time abroad, I suppose? Wished we were there, I suppose?" I was envious. London was sooting me up and I couldn't shed it, layer by layer, like the plane trees in the park.

"You suppose right. They had a terrific time in Brussels on the way back," Helen said. "Fiona says that the center of Brussels is far better than Paris."

The center of Brussels has always been ruined for me by the Belgians: bright red lights and dull gray faces—a Methodist Montmartre. "When is their next big party? Tonight?"

"No," Helen said. "Same night as the *première*. She's asked us to come right after the film. We can take Ruth Fleming and her boy friend."

"Nothing doing. We don't have to go into all that again? Wife-swapping parties, they're . . . oh, I don't know, so bloody earnest." Cushions in front of the lampshades, giggling in the corridors, sleepwalking tunes on the gramophone. Then a stray mating with some neighbor wife you'd have to nod to in the morning. All very well for Eskimos.

Helen had been holding an unlit cigarette in her hand ever since I came back from the walk in the park. While I searched round for a light, futilely, like a moth, she took the heavy table lighter from the pocket of her smock and lit her cigarette. "Whatever else, Fiona Stephens is cheer-

3

ful," she said. "She doesn't let things get her down."

Fiona Stephens was so madly gay that if the mood was on her she could have made a Yogi discontented with his lot. "I don't mind her being cheery," I said, "I just mind what she's cheery about. It's a pretty specialized joke."

"You know we don't have to get involved in that," Helen said. "We could go there early and come away early, the way we did last time. We don't have to get involved."

"You've got a rotten memory. We stood around together like kirk elders, all night. I couldn't make up my mind whether they took me for a sex snob or a welfare worker. Nothing doing. I'm not going. No dice."

"Do you ever stop to think what a hypocrite you are?" Helen asked. "Your inference is pretty obvious isn't it? You're a good, clean-limbed boy and I'm the bad wife, the one who wants to go to a sexy party and kick her heels up." She knew I thought nothing of the kind; this was rhetoric. "You've said I had a rotten memory. What about yours? What about all your cozy little lunches with the girls at the studios? What about all this business of ringing from a phone box and pressing Button A before I could answer, so that you could pretend you were still in your office? And just because I want to go to a party and meet new people . . ."

"I don't think much of the Stephenses' new people, and I don't think Ruth Fleming would take to them, either."

This was intended as a way of avoiding the issue. Our quarrels, the real rows, always began on Saturdays, as this one had. By two or three on Sunday morning, knowing that we could sleep late, we would lie in the dark and make the old accusations to which we knew the old denials, hear the old accusations to which we made the old

4

denials; moving in a pattern of speech and behavior which had become traditional, unrewarding and inevitable as an exhausting folk dance.

"But surely you *know* whether Ruth would like the Stephenses' party?" Helen said. "There's so much *sympathy* between you, isn't there? It's all very cozy in an eerie sort of way. Malcolm Fleming was your friend and now you're so very, very chummy with her."

"Ruth and I were good friends when Malcolm was alive," I said.

Helen stubbed out her cigarette, then twisted it in the ash tray until it burst. It was an act of violence. "Oh, I noticed that," she said. "So did Malcolm. We noticed it all right, we'd have been pretty blind if we hadn't. You and Ruth were always talking across other people, as if they weren't in the room, feeding each other cracks like a pair of comedians. It was a marvelous double act." The conversation was now drifting aimlessly, but dangerously, like a jellyfish.

"You've never talked like that before."

"I never wanted to talk about it," Helen said. "God knows how often I stopped myself from talking about it. I don't suppose you'll give me credit for this but I never tried to get between you and Malcolm. I didn't see him the way you saw him but I knew he was the only friend you cared about."

"Thanks," I said, "thanks very much." We had been over this one so often before and I could never put it across to Helen why Malcolm had meant so much to me, from the time I was nineteen, when I joined the battalion at Rawalpindi in India, with one pip so new and rough and yellow that it wouldn't polish, worn on my old khaki

5

drill uniform from the Indian Military Academy, the uniform which had been dyed "jungle" green and shrunk out of shape in the great dying vat of the reinforcement camp at Deolalli. I had bought an ashplant and acquired a scowl to suit my tam-o'-shanter. I was trying to look like a gentleman and a jungle fighter all at once and talking in the nearest thing to an "officer class" accent which I could superimpose on my strangled Scottish high school voice.

This was a regular battalion of Highland infantry and they made me buy regimental clothing before I was allowed to dine in the mess. Otherwise they were kind, if a little ostentatious, when they showed me how to pass the port, how to recognize a pibroch and to stay quiet while it was played, not to raise a knife until the commanding officer raised his, not to smoke until the King was toasted. For all their delicacy, I had the feeling that they were treating me as an honorary equal in the mess. The men were bayonet-happy brawlers in the old tradition, but I did not like the officers. I lived within my platoon, less of an officer than a senior shop steward, until Malcolm Fleming came back from leave. He was a major with a D.S.O. and a Military Cross. The conventional portrait of the Highland Brigade hero ended there.

He was from Special Service and as much of a misfit in the mess as I was. He avoided the other senior officers and they avoided him. He was an untidy character, walking through the lines with his head in the air and his lips sometimes moving as he tried to cope with the surge of ideas in his head. By that time his last mission to the Karens was well known, but he preferred to talk about books and notions he picked up. He adopted me, he became my *guru*. We were friends from that day. Even now

6

I could remember trying out ideas on him, ideas which he thought preposterous. I could remember his attempts to be grave, then the sudden single-sided grin. . . .

"Who are you thinking about?" Helen asked. "Malcolm or her?"

"Malcolm," I said. "I don't know what you're driving at."

"I think you do," she said. "I think you do. And I'll tell you something. If *you* aren't going to the Stephenses' party, *I* am not going to the film *première* with Ruth Fleming."

So the argument began and it developed through the afternoon and evening into the night. At two, she left the bedroom, taking the electric clock, the electric fire, the electric blanket, all of which she still used when it wasn't cold. I said that she was an electrically minded Bedouin.

"Oh, you can be so *superior*," she said. "Sometimes I actually dislike you. I hate you, I hate you, I hate you."

At three she came back and said, "I'm leaving in the morning."

"I'll go," I said. "You take the flat and all that. I just want my clothes and books."

"*Your* books?" Helen said. "The books we collected together? *Your* books. You, the literate member of the family. Big head. You can leave if you like but I'm not staying here. I'm going to Margot's."

"If you're going, go. Stop threatening. Don't phone your sister to convince *yourself* that you're going, then change your mind. Just go."

We had been through all of this so many times before that I thought it was just another squalid row, at a time when the only passion we could share was anger. She had been twisting her wedding ring; she suddenly freed it and threw it along the bedroom carpet. It rolled for a little, wobbled, then futilely collapsed.

"This time you mean it, don't you?" Helen asked. "This time you really mean it. Well, I mean it, too. Have a marvelous time with Ruth. I'm going." And she went.

2

One result was the embarrassingly empty seat beside me in the circle at the world *première* of *Cry Freedom*. The stars in the film had smiled for the cameras and the shrubbery of eyes beyond the police cordon. They had autographed souvenir programs and recited the alphabet to each other, smiling, while newsreel cameras "caught them in conversation." They had taken their seats, seen their names on the credit titles, waited for the first laughs and gasps from the audience and then slipped out in the darkness, with the silent purpose of a war patrol. But, for me, the only significantly empty seat was the one Helen should have had.

She wouldn't meet me; she wouldn't answer letters or come to the telephone. In the flat everything reminded me of her and I didn't know whether I was suffering for love or from discomfort and the withdrawal of a long-established habit.

On screen, an actor who looked far too sensitive and imaginative to pull a Christmas cracker took the pin from a hand grenade, threw the pin away, then held the grenade with the lever pressed against a Japanese colonel's stomach. If the colonel moved, the grenade would explode.

Grenades always worked like that in films. The sensitive actor was supposed to be Malcolm and he hardly looked the part.

He was a tall, dark, slender flower with a Home Counties and Rank Charm School accent. When he smiled, he was inclined to flutter his eyelashes and show the art work of his dentist. "Now, you ruddy Nip," he said to the colonel. "Stay as sweet as sugar, or you'll never see another teahouse."

There was a lot of laughter at this jest and Randolph, Ruth Fleming's escort, joined in cautiously. While he laughed, Ruth touched the sleeve of my overlight hired dress suit which made me think of ceremonial pajamas. "Sorry I imposed this on you," she said. "The film's a bit grim."

It was typical of Ruth to refuse to play the war hero's widow at a film *première*. There was no disloyalty there, for Malcolm had never thought of himself as a war hero. I couldn't think why he'd had any part in this film, which was planned in the year he died, the year I was abroad. He had disliked the other war films about Burma; he had reckoned it was time the film industry forgave the Japanese, time the audiences who wanted to sit in the cinema and chant "hate, hate, hate" were provided with a less dangerous outlet.

The camera hurtled on through a puce and pea-green jungle, picking out unlikely blossoms from unlikely angles until I felt as if I were swinging, head downward, from the roof of a glasshouse at Kew. Well-known casting agency tribesmen rose and followed the white men against the yellow; trees groaned under improbable weights of vultures and then the monsoon came.

9

The film ended, the great purple curtains closed and a solitary piper in jungle-green drill walked the cinema stage. Like the piper in the film, he had a blood-stained bandage on one arm and parachute silk wrapped round his feet instead of boots, but his trousers were starched and keenly pressed. When he was joined on stage by a full pipe-band, playing "Hielan' Laddie," the audience in the circle rose and, with high heads after their recent ordeal behind the Japanese lines, marched off until they were stopped by other cinema-goers who were counter-marching or marking time in the aisles. Even here, the music made my scalp tingle, my blood glad.

"A peace-loving nation," Ruth said, once we were far enough from the bagpipe rant. "God knows what it would be like if there were ninety million of us Scots in Japan or the middle of Europe."

I was separated from her in the foyer crush. Otherwise I wouldn't have run into Dougal Macphail, the man who got Malcolm Fleming out of Burma. He was probably there as a "guest" of the film company; it was a long journey and an expensive fare from his home on the island of Inish. "A load of bull, eh?" he said, "pitter, pat-ter, oily water. And they pay good money to see the like of that? But you'll admit I died bravely, will you not? I'm happy to know that the Japanese didn't get that dying letter to my mother. I must have been wandering in my mind, right enough. My mother died in 1933. Are you with Mrs. Fleming? I thought as much. You were always a great admirer of her husband."

"I can see her," I said. "She's over there. Come on over."

"Not me," he said, "but I'll see you again, eh? If you're ever up Mallaig way, you'll not pass my door?"

"Don't be daft. Come on and talk to Mrs. Fleming about old times and all that."

"Old times with Major Fleming? I'll tell you something for the first time, Mr. Cameron. Many and many's the time I've wished I'd left that chancer to the Japanese."

Chancer? Liar? Phoney? Romancer?

He turned back into the crowd and moved off fast, while I was still saying, "What do you mean? What the hell do you mean?" He didn't even turn round; he had made a door and vanished while I was still pushing through the crowd, trying to get round a group of starlets, all eyes and gush and borrowed finery, bombarding film executives with their good-bys.

I gave up then and tried to control the hammering anger. Much as I disliked the war film and the war hero cult, I disliked the blood sport of tearing down heroes even more. I didn't want to know that Davy Crockett surrendered at the Alamo, that King Arthur was a local mounted tearaway for the Romans, that T. E. Lawrence was a liar, or that Little Noddy's head wasn't really made of wood.

Above all I couldn't stand attacks on Malcolm Fleming and Macphail must have known that. Perhaps he was disappointed in the small part the man with his name had played in the film; perhaps he was envying dead Malcolm his share of the "glory" and "glamour." As I turned back, I decided to say nothing to Ruth. She had enough on her plate; she was in the small, select gathering which the director of the film was addressing, in the center of the foyer.

I knew the director slightly and I would have gone some way to avoid him. I didn't share his conviction that he was a genius; I did not like his Italian-influenced suits or his long, dark hair which some bespoken barber tended and tried to interpret. He was doing his best to impress Ruth, not, I suspected, because she was the war hero's widow, but because she was easily the best-looking woman in the foyer. She had acquired neither her tan nor her dress at home in Scotland and the length of fashion suited her legs. It was never possible to be anywhere near Ruth without being aware of her legs.

Before I reached them, she twice examined the heels of her shoes. When I got close enough, I saw that her eyes were almost expressionless and her face was very still. If he had known her better, the director would have recognized these signs of boredom. She was controlling everything except her mouth, which was full, sensitive and passionate. At that moment the lips were turning down.

The director nodded to me and plunged on, determined not to be interrupted. Of course it had helped always being interested in the Fleming story. Lot of rubbish written about it since, but he'd always wanted to make it. He was proud, more than proud, when Major Fleming agreed to co-operate with him on it, on something accurate, inspiring. If only Fleming had lived, this would have been quite a moment. He looked at us for confirmation and I began to search for cigarettes while Ruth beachcombed in her evening bag. We reacted at the same time and I remembered Helen's bitter crack about the "double act."

The producer, the money-man of the film, spoke up. "And we made it *without* a best-selling book," he said. "Eh? Think of that. These books, lot of tripe, go for thousands of pounds. And what for? So that you start off from scratch all over again. The people who come to see pictures, they don't read these books. So? You get a good story and you make it, never mind the book, spend the money on your stars, on publicity. The best war stories, none of them ever got to be books. Excuse me." The producer seemed to have convinced himself. He looked a little happier as he walked away.

"I wish I'd known Major Fleming," an elderly woman said. "I didn't know how hard he tried to save Angus." She stopped then and we waited until she felt like going on. This would be Lieutenant Ramsay's mother. Angus Ramsay was killed on that patrol.

"He did," the director said. "He did indeed." He went straight back to his narrative, decorating his speech with pidgin Urdu phrases like "eck dum" and "jungly wallah," overcome with the memory of war and British India, when he was a local, temporary, acting unpaid sahib. There were many like him, bored with the cowardly present, obsessed with war and heroism, revisiting their heroic youth, when they were completely alive, when every day was lived for its own sake. If they had fought in Europe, they would remember a German woman and forget the hunger and the hopelessness, the crumbled cities. If they had been in India, they would remember tonga rides with girls on nights in January and forget the heat, the smells, the crippled beggars, the high and hellish whine of mango flies.

The common preoccupation with war suggested a lack of interest in life, but the director was a special case. This was his fourth war film and, in each, he had refought an action to his own satisfaction, playing the general and the hero at once, vanquishing the enemy and decorating his actors for deeds of valor at a special investiture in Leicester

Square. As he talked on, he made it clear that he, in his Napoleonic imagination, had conducted that last patrol and that Malcolm Fleming and his men had provided only the basic idea, the first treatment. But he thought that he had caught the *feeling* of Fleming and his men. As a matter of fact, he'd had similar experiences himself, in a smaller way of course. . . .

"I thought so," Ruth said. "I felt you caught the wartime atmosphere of Delhi very well." The director looked at her quickly, but she avoided his eye. Ruth had the low, slow, warm voice and the affectedly plain speech of many women of the Scottish moneyed classes. No producer would ever have cast her to make barbed remarks.

"I think we'd better go," her escort, Randolph, said. "This is fascinating but it's getting late. I think we'd better go." I agreed and went to get the car.

"Thanks for protecting me," Ruth said to Randolph as we drove away. "Thanks for saving a scene. The way he cut off Mrs. Ramsay, the swollen-headed fool."

"It's no use crying over spilt milk," Randolph said. "Malcolm agreed to let them make a film; he was paid for his advice. The whole thing's over."

"He got *no* money for it," Ruth said, "not a penny. His fee went to some prisoners-of-war fund."

"No money?" Randolph said. "But why did he do it? He was always complaining about the nonsense newspapers wrote about that patrol. I don't understand."

"I don't know, either," Ruth said. "Malcolm did some odd things before the end. And the last thing I want to talk about now is that film." I thought she was right; we could talk about this some other time, this and what Macphail had said, sometime when Randolph wasn't

14

around. He was moving about in his seat, about to say something.

"Tom," he said at last, "are you . . . eh . . . do you feel . . . will you join us for supper? We're having a meal at a little place I know. It's a pity your wife couldn't make it. We might have made a four."

This was my cue to go and I was just about to take it when Ruth said, "Oh, I don't know about that, Randolph. I'm not hungry. It's getting pretty late and I'm going back early in the morning. Could we drop you? Tom and I? We've a lot of things to talk about. Would you mind?"

"Of course, of course," Randolph said, too heartily, and asked me to drop him at a club I knew well. There I'd often picked up Malcolm when he turned up in London without warning, on what he called a "swan," unintentionally and unselfconsciously using the old Army phrase for a jaunt.

Malcolm in London, for no particular purpose, usually meant that he was quarreling with Ruth again, although he didn't talk about it often. We would go out together and talk about anything but marriage. Sometimes he was inclined to forget that I was no longer nineteen, no longer in such need of a *guru*. When I argued with him, he would often laugh and write off my arguments as "sorehead." But, in terms of friendship, this was small stuff. He was so unlike the bulk of people I knew; particularly in television, newspapers, publishing and the Show Business in general. He was very far from the variety boys who talked and thought in the mental shorthand of the Charing Cross Road; from the soft-faced permanent undergraduates in their middle thirties who lived in little cliques and who were all writing plays; from the hard career girls with

15

their tedious vendettas and weepy love affairs. An evening with Malcolm meant coming up for air.

He would come down depressed, then shake it off, become curious again about life and things. In India, he had been the only officer in the mess who was ever interested in Hindu temples or how Chinese restaurants on the plains managed to get fresh fish. In London, if his head wasn't full of a book, he could absorb himself with a starling flight line or get worked up about the size of the army of cleaners which coped with the London Underground.

"Malcolm's club," I said to Ruth as we left Randolph and drove away.

"Malcolm's club," she agreed. "Where he used to tell you what hell it was being married to me."

"He didn't say much about that."

"I'll take your word for it," she said. "Where are we going?" I told her; it was the nearest Soho place I knew. I'd always wanted to be in *Who's Who* so that I could list all the ten-bob Soho touches I knew, under the heading *Clubs*.

"Oh, gruff, are you?" she asked. "You think I was rude to Randolph, pretty cool?"

"Yes."

"Well, I wasn't. It was kindness. I don't much care for the "little-place-I-know." In the daylight, he's a nice man who sometimes proposes. Anyway, I didn't like the way he tried to drop you overboard," Ruth said. "Stop grinning. You think I'm a ruthless bitch, don't you?"

"Yes."

"That's a pity. I wanted to be sympathetic. I want to know what's wrong between you and Helen. It was so obvious. You were lying your head off."

"I don't know what you mean."

"Come off it," Ruth said. "When you put on that little-boy-lost look, I know you're lying." We had a strange friendship. I had always admired Ruth for her looks, her style, her contempt for little womanly ways and her greater contempt for convention. But, when she was alone, when she didn't have an audience to show how tough she was, she could be very warm and sympathetic. She was almost a year younger than I, but she had played big sister from the first day we met. In thirteen years she had given me some remarkably bad advice.

"When did you ever fool me?" she asked.

"Not very often." I might well have been a third-rate liar but I hadn't spoken to anyone about Helen having left. I'd been evasive and I'd managed to keep up appearances. Nowadays, there are drip-dry shirts, trousers which keep their creases, tinned meals. The more obvious hardships have gone from bachelorhood.

We found a table far enough away from the pair of basement minstrels who had guitars which they could not play and the essential handsome, hungry, amateur look. The great appeal of this music was the do-it-yourself appeal and the great danger was that they were dragging the guitar down with them at the end, into years of oblivion now that rock and skiffle were almost over. They wouldn't care. They would happily play pitch pipes if Ancient China was in fashion.

"All right," Ruth said, again, "let's have it." Very soon she had me talking. I'd always found it easier to talk to her about things which worried me than to any other person, even Malcolm, even Helen. Once, all hell broke loose when Helen found out that I'd asked her advice about my job.

"The main trouble with you has always been that you

17

haven't any children," Ruth said, when I had finished. "The rest of it is a lot of nonsense. Why didn't you ever do anything about that?"

"I don't know," I said. "Anyway, it's too late now." Helen had been in hospital for a check and they reckoned we could have children, after all. But she was hardly out before our rows began again and she'd said that having a child was a woman's-magazine solution.

Ruth was beginning to question me when we were interrupted. "Evening, Cameron," my neighbor Stanley said. Of all the places in Soho, my neighbor Stanley and his wife had chosen this one for their late night hot chocolate or whatever it was they drank. Stanley was a fat little man with a melodramatically okay voice, with restless eyes and limp dark clothing. His face resembled a child's drawing of a cow's face, even to the small, ill-placed eyes. He was a born nark, a Sherlock Holmes enthusiast, a frustrated amateur detective. I did not like him.

"Good evening," I said. "Good evening, Mrs. Stanley." I did not introduce Ruth.

"Going to the Stephenses' party?" he asked.

"No."

"Neither are we." I tried to look surprised but I was certain that they had not been asked. Stanley was one of the few subjects on which Phillip Stephens and I agreed. "I saw your wife today," Stanley added, after his wife and Ruth had exchanged the quick, brilliant smile of women who dislike each other on sight.

I said nothing and the conversation lagged.

"Well . . ." Mrs. Stanley said, at last.

"Yes, of course. I'm sorry but we'll have to toddle on," her husband answered. They walked to the door, where

Stanley chatted with the doorkeeper, who bent and listened, withdrawn but polite. Stanley had a deep, doggy desire to be liked. I realized too late that I should have introduced Ruth and given him a full account of the evening.

"I'm in real trouble now," I said to her. "By this time tomorrow, Helen will know that we were sitting in this whisky-scented twilight, talking quietly, nose to nose. This was the night I was supposed to be at a *première* with you and Randolph."

Helen was bound to hear of it and I thought of all the unlikely stories with which I had bombarded her in our troubled past. Once when I found myself indoors without the beginnings of a plausible story, I had even said, "The most awful thing. I almost ran over a cyclist." But I wouldn't have expected her to believe that I was sitting in a "club," alone with Ruth at this time of night, getting advice on how to get my wife back. I wouldn't have expected a yak to believe that.

"I ought to pretend to be surprised," Ruth said. "I always made a point of not noticing that Helen thought I was trying to pinch you from her."

"That's a bit strong," I said, "but I should have talked to Stanley about the film. I should have said that Randolph had just nipped out for a while." Ruth looked at me closely. She was trying to control her mouth. When she spluttered, she put her hand over it.

"You would have said something like that, wouldn't you?" she asked. "You would have done your best and given Stanley the idea that you and I were the most hammy pair of plotters since Guy Fawkes? You really are a lousy liar. What was the party he was talking about?"

19

I was surprised to find myself defending the Stephenses' gang to her, arguing that they were often pleasant individuals and only offensive in the mob.

They were all suffering from the Sidney Court complaint: they all felt that they were riding too close to forty or thirty-five or whatever age group the couple involved thought was the "dangerous age." They wanted to live, wanted to have fun and games without the risk, without "cheating," without "deception." They wanted to break the rules and still remain safe. You can't tell on me because you did it too. Oh yes, you did.

"It must sound pretty drab to you and pretty squalid," I said. "One thing though, they aren't rich, like you. They can't go where they like, when they like. They're lonely and, in our belt, loneliness can have some pretty distressing symptoms."

I gave her an example, Maisie Morris.

When she first came to the Court, Maisie Morris had decided that there was a higher society among us than the Stephenses' gang. In her attempts to crash this imaginary high society, she had given sticky tea parties for the children and lavish dinners for their parents. She had frightened away the parents by entertaining in a way they couldn't afford and by a habit she had of telling the same anecdotes after every dinner. When she began the old, old story, her husband would rise to wash dishes, or put on coal, or just to hide in a bedroom until it was over. Maisie was still convinced that there was a higher society from which she was excluded. She made up for it by being the boldest guest the Stephenses had, dancing with abandon, turning a tango into a fertility rite. Her husband stood round the fringe of the parties, picking quarrels.

"Do you think you have to tell me about loneliness?" Ruth asked. She was swirling the liquid in her glass and looking down into it. "Or what it does to you?"

Loneliness for her, she said, was the loneliness of being with women friends who had husbands and whose lives were their husbands, women who regarded her not simply as bereaved but as crippled. They were tactful, they didn't even complain about their husbands any more, they stuck to safe topics like clothes and idle charwomen. Loneliness meant being with men like Randolph, who felt their male responsibilities to a widow of a friend, always. They either had to try to protect her, or to marry her, or to make her. "I'm just over thirty," Ruth said, "and there isn't a wide choice of men in my age group and I'm a damned sight more choosey than I was at seventeen. I would look round for somebody at the right marrying age, somebody about twenty-five. But I can't stand the thought of being fifty in that kind of setup, wearing young women's skirts, knowing the diet sheets by heart, getting all dewy at the mouth at the third or fourth drink, and patting young boys' knees to make your husband jealous." I knew she was thinking of her mother's life.

Loneliness meant having coffee on the fourth floor of a big store in her town, watching greedy women dissecting cakes and realizing she was getting like them. "There's nothing wrong with having money," Ruth said. "I'm not fooling myself about that. But maybe it would have been better if I'd been a plucky little widow who had to do a job. But what could I make? A tenner a week? A job's fine if you need the money, but it's a pretty damned silly hobby. I'm sorry, I'm sorry. I shouldn't have started off on this. We're on your troubles." She emptied my matchbox on the table and began to build a house of matches. Her fingers shook. When Ruth was intense, she was very intense. She enjoyed her violent swings of mood.

"What about Jill?" I asked. Jill was her small daughter.

"Oh, Jill," she said. "Yes, Jill." She built a roof on the house, jerked a support and the whole thing collapsed. "Jill's pretty young," she said. "I try not to lean too much on her. Honestly, I try. She's a nice child and it's a bit rough for her, providing warmth and love for me and my mother, and Malcolm's parents all at once. I'm not going to make her my sister, my chum, in her first year at school. That's what my mother did to me."

The guitarist came over with his collection hat, looked long at Ruth on his way across, held out his hat to me while he gave her his most brilliant Teddy-without-a-Cause smile. I dropped a half-crown into his hat, with menace. Ruth did not miss this byplay and she was pleased.

"You could move," I said, "make a change, come to London."

"I couldn't live here," she said. "That stuff about wife-swapping parties, that frightens me. That's loneliness, without any good reason for being lonely, people acting stupidly because they've lost their sense of who they are and what they stand for in this great big, anonymous place. Do you know what somebody once called London? A caricature of infinity. I can cope with our town; it's small. Why don't you come back sometime? Don't you think a holiday at home would do you good?"

The obvious way to spend a month off was here in London, trying to patch things up, but I had the feeling that I couldn't patch things up with Helen, whatever

22

Ruth said, and I was tired of living this way, on a marginal standard of reality. If I went home to Scotland, it would be no more than a retreat from problems, even an attempt to retreat from myself. Well then, to hell with it; sound the retreat. *Piper, play "Bundle and Go."* I was feeling better for Ruth's company, a lot better, and she would be gone in the morning. "I'll do that," I said. "I'll come home. And right now, I'd better take you back to your hotel."

It had been raining and my tourer wouldn't start, so I got out and reached for the starting handle which always lay on the back seat, at the ready like a Pony Express rifle. As I maneuvered it out the handle struck the lowest part of the sagging hood and the released rainwater ran gratefully down my neck.

"Better night now," Neighbor Stanley said, coming up suddenly out of the dark, with his wife. By one of those breathtaking coincidences, which only involve people like Stanley, he happened to have been waiting there, trying to hail a taxi. "Rain won't be back tonight," he said, with a confident ring in his voice.

I agreed quickly, trying to fit the starting handle, preferring to leave meteorological speculation to the dedicated campers on the Air Ministry roof.

"Cold car in wet weather, I suppose?" he went on. "Bit unpleasant for your wife when the summer's over, won't it?"

His wife was peering in, humming to herself, looking at Ruth while she lit a cigarette which she had taken from the glove pocket, indicating that she was thoroughly familiar with the car.

"You could make modifications, I suppose," he said,

"make it warmer in winter for your wife?"

"Yes," I said, "it's quite simple, nothing to it. We're having a built-in brazier in the back." I started the car with a single, vicious swing.

When I dropped Ruth, I went home. It was a warm night, windows were open all along Sidney Court and the Stephenses were insulting the memory of Glenn Miller with a rendering of "I've Got You Under My Skin." I was restless, I kept thinking of Helen, I wanted company. But the only friend I had in the Court who was likely to be awake was the porter and he was anxious and remote at this time. Ever since the Rent Act, the owners had been smartening him up for the richer, younger tenants who had moved in, having been evicted from Chelsea, and who were, in turn, sending the older, poorer Sidney Court tenants wandering to Bayswater, or Earls Court or to lingering death in the southern suburbs.

The owners had even made the porter sign a new, long agreement over a sixpenny stamp. One of the duties on the agreement was that he would "parade the grounds between six and seven-thirty in the provided uniform." The only items of uniform so far provided were a peaked cap and two shirts. He wasn't certain whether to be disobedient or obscene. It wasn't fair to bother him at such a time.

Thought drifted on to Malcolm and the film. There was something wrong; I had known there was something wrong, long before Sergeant-Major Macphail's words at the film *première*, something so far wrong that I'd conveniently forgotten to ask Ruth about it.

I went to my desk where an old typewriter was waiting

24

for a ribbon. In the bottom drawer there were letters which had been waiting longer to be answered. It didn't take long to find the one I wanted, an old letter from Malcolm.

He had been complaining about the war memoirs in the Sunday papers and he went on:

I'll tell you why the British are interested in building up war heroes—because we didn't show up too well in the last war, compared with the characters on the other side . . . the boys fighting for rotten causes. Do you know how many Japanese prisoners the British had taken by the beginning of 1945? Fourteen. And some of them asked to be killed when they were captured. They were so ashamed, not like us at all.

The British were shaken rigid by the way that trapped, doomed German Army fought at Stalingrad. They were really shaken when they got the last letters from Stalingrad, the letters that showed these men weren't fanatics, weren't zombies.

If you want to get a general idea of how the British fought this war look at the way we used ammunition in Germany. Did you know that, from Normandy to Bremen, we used 1,000 rounds of artillery shells for every rifle shot we fired? We weren't hellish keen on close combat.

The British know about that, deep down they know about that. But they can't have foreigners pinching their traditional boneheaded values. So they make gods of the little warlords with long memories, from the twopence halfpenny, no-account side shows. . . .

I didn't think it was one of his better theories, but he seemed sincere. It was odd that a man who thought like that should let himself become the hero of a war film about a "no-account side show." It was very odd.

3

Weeks passed, Helen stayed away and I went walking in the drafty dark of Studio C, our head man's favored studio. "Television," our head man always said. "It's Television. We have to get it right. We owe it to the viewers." He spoke with a simple conviction, he had one god, Television, and he was Television's Prophet.

At eight that night the program "Dreams Come True" would be on the air and by four in the afternoon his favorite C studio was beginning to be lit and warmed by camera crews, floor assistants, prop men, all looking as if they preferred to believe that television did not exist. I nodded in sympathy to people I knew. A makeup girl smiled and, from force of habit, checked my brow for shine. Sound came on and from the heights of the studio, recorded voices sang the signature tune of "Dreams Come True."

> Always I've dreamed my dreams,
> In cities and by mountain streams,
> Are you the answer to my prayer?
> Can you help me, help me,
> You down there?
> Make my dearest dream come true?

A scriptwriter was penciling in the last pleasantries of spontaneous dialogue for this live, unrehearsed show, due on the air in five hours' time. "Where's Sam?" I asked, and he jerked his pencil in the general direction of the rehearsal room. On the way I passed a "Roman" set. There one of the studio assistants was practicing throwing a weight into a zinc tub on a given signal, the noise to suggest a coin being tossed with a wish into a Roman fountain. Even to heat and light and fill a studio such as this on the air would cost all of £1,000 an hour, but, to keep within his budget, the producer had to rely on a throw, perfectly timed by a nonathletic parasite who didn't look as if he understood the principle of ducks and drakes. This was television all right.

In the rehearsal room, Sam Winters was vetting potential "members of the studio audience" for likely faces on which the camera could dwell at tense moments in the program. At a first glance, all of these possibles looked as if they might have shuffled out of a documentary about the march from Jarrow in the hollow thirties. The compère of "Dreams Come True" believed in pathos. He had to convince his viewers of the universality of suffering.

"Hullo, cocker," Sam said. "Give me a minute." He turned to an assistant. "Get rid of the studio audience for now. And we can't have Shirley Choate in the audience again."

"Why not?" the assistant asked. "Shirley Choate's a nice old girl. Marvelous surprised face."

"I can't have her," Sam said. "I like her, too, but her face is getting too well known. And her agent's getting above himself. He wants more for her, reckons that she's an 'atmosphere' actress now. Same all through television. Everybody fighting for promotion, trying to reach the limelight. The bloody callboy on this program's started to call himself a liaison officer. Come on, Tom. Quick cup of coffee."

Sam glanced at his watch, his self-winding, shockproof,

heat-defying watch, which was capable of withstanding water pressure down to thirty-three feet, perhaps in case he was suddenly summoned to produce a piece of underwater ballet. "We'll have to be quick," he said. The producer's box was a torture chamber for him. He would sit there, mesmerized by the movement of the second hand of the clock, persuaded that nothing would be right when the moment came. He suffered from the recurring nightmare that his cameras would go on musth and stampede out of the studios at the second he was due on the air.

Now he could relax for the time it took to drink a cup of coffee, but, for the first few minutes, he complained about the commercials in the natural breaks in his program. Sam's theory was that good commercials helped a show but that his was always ruined by stuff about headaches and laxatives. "Now is *that* entertainment?" he asked. "Why can't they put all that medical muck in the middle of one of these hospital programs, put it in the natural breaks between shrieks? I'm beginning to think that these bloody advertisers have no souls. If I wasn't such a bloody snob, I'd join the B.B.C." This subject could easily outlast his coffee break and I asked him bluntly if he had seen Helen, for she was a close friend of Sam's wife.

"I'm not supposed to tell you," he said, at once. "She made me promise that I wouldn't tell you she was over."

"When?"

"Oh, she came round last night. I'm sorry, but I think you've had it, chum." I thought of Sam as a happily married man. His expression suggested not sympathy, but envy.

"You don't look very sorry," I said.

"Maybe not," he said. "And if you're going to end up

28

divorced, don't go round telling too many of us happy, cozy couples. You could start off a chain reaction. All it needs is a start among our lot and anything could happen."

He was always anxious about his poorer jokes, inclined to look immediately for an audience reaction. "I'm sorry, Tom," he said, after a moment. "I shouldn't have said that. You don't look very happy. What you're needing is a holiday. Get away somewhere and think. Your eyes are so bloody bloodshot that they look like surrealistic marbles. Take a tip, chum. Leave Helen alone; it's your only chance. Let her do some thinking too. You're needing a rest from this place; you're getting stale. What sort of rating did you get for your last program?" I held both thumbs down. I didn't mind so much about the rating. The weaker intellects among our management are inclined to suspect that a poor rating for a documentary program means that it was a good documentary program. But the critics had chewed me up, even the literate television critics had chewed me up.

"Don't worry," Sam said. "All you're needing is a holiday. All this 'significant' television is killing you." He often said that he would do anything for television so long as it wasn't harmful or "significant." According to Sam, television's only "significant" achievement was to cut down the suicide rate in lonely areas.

"Don't worry," he said again, "and, for Christ's sake, stop drumming on the table." I lifted my hand quickly. This was a mannerism which I thought I'd lost. "You're so bloody taut that you make me feel relaxed," he said.

"The nerve quacks would make a fortune out of characters in television . . . if we only earned any money."

Sam looked at his watch again and I knew that he had

no more time for private thought. He was swaying forward on the dangerous flood of television that never sleeps or dies and, held one moment, burns the hand.

There was a crackle overhead and the loud-speaker came to life. "Mr. Winters," it said, "will Mr. Winters take a call?"

On the way back to my office, I passed through a private audience research group, amateurs come to announce their findings to the cowering professionals. They were so radiant with anticipation and self-importance that I felt that I was passing through a cloud of comet dust.

Sam would have made some perverse remark but I envied them their enthusiasm. I couldn't forget that I must have looked like that myself when I first walked these corridors, in the days when I thought I'd found something to believe in, when I found that the people who count in television are never as cynical, as politically amoral or as contemptuous of their customers as people in other branches of communication are. I didn't know where I'd lost that feeling, or when, or why. There was no good reason. It certainly wasn't because of the critics who ignored the public hunger for simple knowledge and said, "Let them eat culture."

Probably I'd lost it because I'd never believed in anything for long. Certainly Helen's theory didn't hold water. She'd always argued that Malcolm had a lot to do with my lost enthusiasm, that he had slowly kidded me out of it. She said that Malcolm had argued that I was being led up the garden path, that once they were in their true position of power the contractors would rid themselves of all the enthusiasts and get themselves hatchet men.

This, all of this, would certainly have fitted into Mal-

30

colm's basic theme that we were moving into dark authoritarian times; however much the liberal might rave and rant. But I didn't remember him saying that, and I couldn't think why I should agree with him, if he had. I didn't believe, as Helen did, that Malcolm would want to make me feel futile in my job, because he felt futile in his.

Whatever it was, it had happened and there was no point in blaming any other man. A journalist once wrote, "Show me a cynic in television and I'll show you a failure." He was talking about Sam Winters and me.

I was reminded of that again later in the afternoon when I called on Maitland, my boss in Documentaries, to ask for a holiday. I had been dodging him for a bit. Maitland had done a lot for me and, lately, I hadn't done very much for him. He was a short, trim, brisk character, with a tapering skull, a high-winged collar and hair which had been long enslaved by brush and grease. "All right," he said, "where do you want to go?"

"Scotland."

"It suits me," he said. "It couldn't be better if you went right away. I'm going to need you badly in about six weeks. Do you think you can take a bit of advice?" He swung round in his swivel chair and put his feet up. When Maitland put his highly polished black shoes on his desk and looked relaxed, we automatically expected trouble, but I respected his judgment and his advice rather more than I disliked the way he expressed them. I nodded, cautiously.

"Have a lot of early nights and good long walks," he said. "You're letting this place get on top of you. You're getting mixed up with the brittle boys, the cynics, the knockers. You're always telling me you don't like them but you attract them like a magnet . . . people like Sam Winters, for instance. They're teaching you to be terrified of sincerity. Nowadays you don't want to show a foot of film which isn't clever—clever and slanted—which doesn't give a horselaugh at some poor fool being interviewed. Roughly, your attitude is 'I have many human friends, but—' "

That more or less summed up what the critics had said about my last program. "It sounds as if I might as well go away for good," I said. "You make me sound like somebody in a Horlick's ad."

Maitland grinned. "You look like somebody in a Horlick's ad," he said, "but did you ever see a Horlick's advertisement with an unhappy ending? I've got something for you, a big job. You're going to need a lot of deep, refreshing sleep." He threw across the memo. By this time, thanks to Sam, my troubles were known throughout the firm. Maitland, the sadistic swine, had switched me to make six half-hour programs on the subject of divorce.

I couldn't reach my brother by phone, so I sent him a telegram to say I was coming home, then I left early to pack. On the way I dropped into the studio club, where staff people and privileged outsiders were clothing themselves in an alcoholic veil against the evening. There I found Willie Greenhill, whom I hadn't met for weeks. Willie was a real television enthusiast, with all of the sincerity which Maitland said was frightening me.

He produced uncommitted plays with lines which sounded like a skit on Eugene O'Neill, with fading film stars in the principal parts and bit players who clung stubbornly to the Method. The action was so slow that

Sam Winters said we could put on *King Lear* straight afterward, as a leg-show. Willie had a habit of getting down on his knees at rehearsals and imploring the actors to play it *seriously*, to *him*. He was that rarity in our time, a happy, integrated eccentric.

"Hullo, Tom," he said, "sorry you weren't at the Stephenses' party." The Stephenses' party didn't sound right for him. He was a Zen Buddhist and Sam said that Willie hoped to end up as Head of Religious Broadcasts.

"The Stephenses' party?" I asked. "What were you doing at the Stephenses' party?"

"Looking for atmosphere, of course," he said. "You hear a glass falling in a bedroom, you know? Then melodramatic moaning? Pretty sordid but a useful piece of background for *The Small Gilded Fly*."

I knew that he badly wanted me to ask what *The Small Gilded Fly* was, so I asked him.

"Oh, a play, you know?" he said, and quoted in a quick, self-conscious mumble, " 'Die for adultery! No: The wren goes to't, and the small gilded fly does lecher in my sight.' Oh, that reminds me. Your wife was at the party and she cut me dead. I've been meaning to ask you what I'm supposed to have done."

"She wouldn't cut you dead, Willie. It would be a mistake; she's a bit shortsighted." Willie was worried enough about personal relationships without Helen adding to it. "And of course she would be busy, helping Fiona Stephens; cutting sandwiches, helping with drinks and so on."

"I suppose so," Willie said. "It could have been that. Maybe that's what she was doing."

4

In Ruth's flat, I opened the wine bottle with a stainless steel contraption which seemed designed to grind the cork into the wine with six swift, patented movements.

"Will you carve?" she asked. She watched me for a bit, then she said, "No, no, no. Steady up. I'll do it. You've still got ten thumbs instead of fingers." She looked at the savaged meat. "Ach, well," she said, "it's better than it was the first time."

I first tried to carve for her when I came home from India on a Python leave, when Malcolm had asked me to take some Kashmiri skirts home for his wife. I didn't think I knew his wife, but I remembered who she was the moment I saw her. I had known her by sight from the time I was fourteen or fifteen. She had been one of the rich girls of the town and by far the best-looking, in a wild way. Often, over the wall, I'd watched her play tennis, laughing at and sometimes throwing her racket at one of the boys back from the Scottish public schools, the boys with the comical accents, who said "Pess the ball, Sendy," and somehow kept their assurance.

"You were so brown," Ruth said now, "so shy and earnest and awkward, a koala bear in a kilt."

"You weren't exactly a society hostess, yourself."

I had called with the skirts, with my kilt cutting the knee in half in regimental fashion and toothpaste on my parachute wings to make them conspicuous. I had expected that Malcolm's wife would be the brigadier's daughter type, of horsy height, flag-down-at-sunset in her loyalty to the regiment. And here was Ruth, the red-haired girl, the wild one, a girl I'd often remembered when we were chasing bandage-faced nurses in Rawalpindi. This was the first time I had ever been consciously jealous of Malcolm. He had too much; this wasn't fair.

"Anyway," I said, "I wouldn't have been so damned awkward if you hadn't held a mannequin parade with the skirts."

"I had to do something," she said. "You were so pie when you were talking about Malcolm. I got the general impression that Mountbatten was his batman. But your carving saved the day, Tom. You could have gone on the halls as a carver."

She had tried very hard to keep her face straight while I carved the first bird she'd been able to buy in months. Then she began to fight down laughter, to choke and splutter. At first I was humiliated, then I joined her. She had a crazy, infectious laugh and she intended no unkindness. We drank a lot and ended at a pub up the river out of town, with Ruth playing elder sister for the first time.

Long before closing time, I was telling her all about the girl I had been writing to in London and the rotten time we'd had since I came back on leave. The girl had gone home to London that very day, for it wasn't working out.

I'd get over the girl, Ruth had said, I didn't really *know* the girl anyway. For years she had been no more than a photograph and a weekly letter. Keep her letters, Ruth said, put them away somewhere, then take them out again in two years' time and read them before you burn them. You'll find that they're far shorter than you remembered and pretty trivial. They always are, written to someone vague and far away. When you've read them again, then burned them, Ruth said, that will be the end of the affair. When you're young and romantic, Ruth said, when you feel that you aren't feeling enough, not sufficiently involved in anything, you reach out for some dramatic situation, trying to force yourself and the people round you into feeling something powerful, just as a hysteric does. I found out later that Ruth used the word hysteric to cover any mental abnormality.

But you'll get over it, Ruth said, you'll get involved another dozen times before you marry. And now drink up, drink up and to hell with drama, Ruth said.

"But your carving wasn't half as rough as your vanishing act," Ruth said now, in her flat.

We had arranged to meet the next day and all night long I thought of her, at home; my parents were still living at that time. It was preposterous to fall in love with Malcolm Fleming's wife. I wrote her a thank-you note and put it through her letter box on my way to the railway station in the morning, when I left for London. She was right about the girl's letters. They *were* pretty trivial, as trivial as the letters I had written to her. But I didn't burn them. They were written by Helen, who became my wife.

"We must go back to that pub one day," Ruth said, "when you've time, I mean. It's a long time since you've been here. You'll have to do an awful lot of visiting and drink an awful lot of tea."

"That's what I thought," I said, "but it's the Fair Week. Trust me to come home in the Fair Week. Bill's away and all my aunties and uncles and cousins, and friends-through-marriage and friends-through-drink are out of town." My old music mistress had stopped me in the High Street and it turned out that she had forgiven me for everything. I had met my old scoutmaster and he reminded me of the time we went searching together for twigs when there was mince for forty on the fire and the wood-pile was perilously low. That was about all. My brother Bill hardly ever leaves town. When I sent the telegram I had automatically assumed that he'd be there.

"Look," Ruth said, "I don't give a damn what people think. You can move in here when you like but it's up to you. If Helen heard about it, there would be all hell to pay. Have you heard from her yet?"

I told her that I hadn't, other than indirectly, through the bank. When Helen stopped drawing checks on our joint account, she meant business.

"That sounds more like a show of strength to me," Ruth said. "I think that's promising, honestly I do. I think that she'll take you back once you've suffered enough. I'll give you one tip, though. When you write to her, she won't be interested in how guilty you feel, what a bad conscience you have. Husbands always make that mistake. Show that you love her, that's all. Poor Tom, you never have to look for trouble, do you?"

"Trouble seeks its own level all over the world," I said. "Wait a minute. What's that?" My sub-television repartee had been interrupted by the sound of something falling.

"Damn, damn, damn," Ruth said. "When the meal's on the table. That's Jill. I promised her you'd go in and say good night. Sorry, I thought she'd forgotten, thought she'd be asleep by now."

Jill's bed was empty, a pillow and several blankets had been removed. She sat on the pillow in her canvas house or tent, in a pool of light from a torch. Jill's hair had recently been cut and the shape of the hair emphasized the size of the eyes, the soft line of the face, neck and chin. She had a bear last known as Boris which had frequent changes of sex and which was now dressed as a nurse. As she rocked the bear in her arms, she sang very quietly, "Your eyes are the eyes of a teddy in love." Jill knew that I was in the room, I knew by the way she adjusted the blanket round her shoulders, but I waited until my presence was acknowledged. "You know, you know," she said politely, "you walk very quietly for a man."

I lifted a window flap of her canvas house. "If you go back to bed this minute," I said, "I won't tell Mummy we used to play the fruit machines at the Funfair. And I'll play cushion fights with you and let you win."

She seemed staggered by this weight of generosity; she said, "You promised and a promise is a promise is a promise," as she got into bed, with an armful of animals. "Tell me a story," Jill said.

"There's a place called Sleepy Time Village. Ever heard of it?" She shook her head, slowly, suspiciously, probably suspecting the purpose behind this story and getting ready to howl that she needed a drink or a cough sweet or the big light on, or her mother, or whatever might seem the best tactic.

"Well, Sleepy Time Village is run by the Sandman and all the boys are sand boys and all the girls are sand girls. Do you know what game they play?"

"What do they wear?"

"Pajamas and dressing gowns and slippers, of course. Do you know what game they play?"

"What game?"

38

"Seeing who can get to sleep first and sleep the longest."

"Well, I know another village where they play a better game; they play at seeing who can wake up first."

"I never heard of that village. I think you're making that up. In Sleepy Time Village they play at seeing who can get to sleep first." I had imagined that she was slowly settling. Now she sat up and spoke loudly.

"And do the girls always win?" she asked.

"Yes." I was thinking of Helen. "In most games I know, the girls *always* win."

"How do you know? You haven't got a girl. You haven't even got a boy."

"No."

"Why not?"

"Some people aren't lucky, that's all. What do you call the teddy bear?"

"Doris," she said, "and some children haven't got a Daddy, unfortunately. My Daddy's gone away, unfortunately." She was waiting for me to confirm this and I couldn't think of anything to say.

"I expect he's in Africa or China or somewhere," she said. "I wonder what he'll bring me. I don't know, unfortunately. I expect you know. I expect you know where he is."

I was shaken by all of this. "Where did you get this word 'unfortunately?'" I asked.

She said, "I made it up." Then I told her another story and eventually got her to sleep.

"What's this about Malcolm being 'away'?" I asked Ruth, while we cleared up.

"Did she talk to you about that? I didn't want you to know. I don't know what to do about it, either. Malcolm's father started it. He didn't mean any harm, to begin with. He was just being evasive on the day Malcolm died."

"But you've told her?"

"Of course I've told her. But she keeps coming back to it, oh, often, after she's seen his parents. I'm getting her away to my mother for a bit. They're always giving her God talk, too. I want her out of their way."

"But can't you talk to his parents, make them see sense?"

"You don't know about that? I don't get on with Malcolm's parents."

"I'm sorry. I didn't know."

"Don't worry. Just don't let's talk about it."

Her mouth was trembling, the skin was suddenly tight around her cheeks and I didn't know what to do. I reached forward and rubbed her temple gently with my knuckles, as if she were a horse. Then I was aware of the idiocy of this; I began to stroke her hair.

"Don't," she said, jerking her head away, "don't do that. That's dangerous." I left early and stayed away for the next few days exploring the town.

My home town is an old town with wide streets and square stone houses on a slow, bold sweep of river. It is near enough the East Coast for the wind to be keen and the joke to come from the side of the mouth. It is within easy reach of Edinburgh, Perth or Dundee and yet close enough to the hills to be one of the fourteen Scottish boroughs which describes itself as "The Gateway to the Highlands."

It was fine being there by day but the evenings were dull. The locals firmly believe that all the people of Arbroath are sly or, as we say, "fly"; that the people of Forfar are "coarn-chaisty," which is a local form of "corny";

that Dundee is dirty and ugly and that Glasgow is worse —a place where one child in every three is of Irish Catholic extraction, a Papist ready for the razor gangs. Edinburgh is not bad, not bad at all. There is one other place in the world and that is our town. But even the locals will not deny that our town is "quiet" at night.

My last evening there alone was long. I wrote to Helen, read the letter carefully, then tore it up. There were three sentences she could misconstrue if she really tried. Then I picked up the book I'd borrowed from Ruth, a paperback edition of an acknowledged master work. But I was confused by the sentence *She was a mountain peak whom all might tread but whom the snows made nightly virginal.* It made me think the chaste heroine of the book had suddenly become a nymphomaniac, a frigid tart. This, I realized, was the worst of being a lewd, frustrated lower middle brow.

At half past eight I gave up and went out to a pub which local golfers used. "Tom Cameron," one of them said. "Has living in London cured your slice yet? What will you drink?" He drew me into the circle of clubhouse wags.

" 'Go to my uncle's funeral?' she says. 'No, no, Andy, you wouldnae enjoy it.' "

" 'Get married?' I says. 'Me? Give a woman half your food so that she'll cook the other half?' "

"Oh, it's fast, his car, real fast. When he gets weaving, the dashboard ash tray does three thousand revs."

I was enjoying all this until Jim Carnegie came in, jerked his head to one side and said, "Hai." This is a traditional local greeting. We had been in the same class at school and he still wore a former pupil tie, his certificate of privilege, his badge of literacy. At school he had been

41

a sneak and a toady, nicknamed the Nyaff. Rugby practice often deteriorated while this child was carefully kicked in the scrum. Even now his face looked as if it had been stamped on swiftly, while it was still hot.

"And you're in television now, I hear?" he asked.

The conversation round us stopped. Television is still a magic word in our town. Men who had been treating me as a fellow rabbit golfer until now looked at me intently, as if a closed-circuit program would start up on my brow.

"Yes."

"And you're living in London?"

"Yes."

"And you like London, then?"

"Very much," I said, forgetting how I'd felt about London a few days before, forgetting the laws of our town. There you can admit a love of New York or Peking or even Moscow. To admit a liking for London is almost as treacherous as attacking the legend of the Scottish fighting man.

Earning a living in London was an amiable eccentricity, at best, tolerable only if you would admit that London was a sprawling dirty place which gave a man a headache the moment he stepped on the Underground, that the prices there were ridiculous, the food poor and suspect, that the English had no sense of humor and that the only point of living in the south was to be able to put a bit by, against retirement and a bungalow just outside our home town, not far from the golf course.

From here men went out across the world but they had to believe that our town was the only worth-while place to live; that the Scots, few though they were, were the only worth-while nation; that the point of all the

42

wandering and all the work was to come back, see our home town again and die.

"So you like London? Fancy that," Carnegie said, looking round. "And you're doing all right, then?"

"No," I said, forgetting again. "I'll be singing for pennies at Charing Cross Tube Station any day now." The golfers were silent again. It is not seemly to joke about success in our town. It is a town where every mother's son is better educated than every other mother's son, and equipped for the battle of life. Our town worships success and this was blasphemy. I finished my beer and left.

Outside the pub I saw a motorist from our hotel stop to ask his way from two policemen and I ran toward them. A strange motorist who stops and smiles and asks the road to somewhere, with the smell of beer on his breath, is not necessarily drunk. He is, in our town, if he asks the way in an effeminate Southern English accent. In our town all Southern English accents are effeminate. A motorist ignorant enough not to know this may also be ignorant enough to ask the way from a policeman. The policeman will return his smile and say, "I'll just get in beside you, mister, and guide you on your road."

He will then sit beside the driver, chatting, affably enough, about the weather and the golf, directing him all the while to the police station. There the motorist will be examined by Dr. Scrimgeour, the police surgeon, who gives every impression of impartiality. How is the motorist to know that Scrimgeour is a fanatic, with temperance posters up on his surgery walls?

Before I reached them, a policeman got into the car. He was grinning as they drove off. The motorist probably mistook it for a smile.

"How do you know he's drunk?" I asked the other policeman. "Do you have to know the town plan by heart to prove sobriety?"

The policeman stroked his small mustache. I knew him, too well. "Have you no eyes in your head?" he asked. "Did you not see him just now? He overtook another car on the near side."

"It's common in London, especially when the other car is doing ten miles an hour in the middle of the road."

"This is not London. A while off the road, with his car in the garage, will teach that man a bit of patience. Where are you off to now, Mr. Cameron?"

"For a drink. I'm a free-born Scottish pedestrian."

"Are you now? Have you a hip flask or something? It's after nine and the public houses are closed. If you're thinking of making a fool of yourself, you'd better go to the dancing."

At nine in our town, returned travelers and other lonely men go to bed or to the local dance hall, the only place which has official sanction to be cheerful until eleven. At the Palais that night there might well have been a river pilot from the Hoogly, a doctor who had handled cholera in Bhopal, a policeman who had tracked down elephant poachers or been ambushed by diamond smugglers in Sierra Leone. They came home gaily but their leaves were long. If there were any such men of the world around, they would be at the bar behind the bandstand looking distinguished and sunburned, swigging orangeade.

Danger or no danger, there was only one place to be in our town at that time of night. There was only one person who did not make me feel a stranger in my home town. I rang Ruth.

44

5

She was nervous when she came to pick me up; she
drove away too fast. The windscreen wipers were screech-
ing noisily on dry glass and the clear crescent in the dust
suggested that they had been on since she left her flat.
As the car cornered, a small black box was driven out of
the way, bleating and honking pitifully.

Her nervousness did not show in her face or her movements; her gear changes were hard and deliberate, like a
man's. She was doing sixty when we went into the bends
along the river. "Change down, honey," I said. "The pits
are signaling. There's a man in the cells tonight for far less
than this."

"I'm sorry," she said, and took her foot off the accelera-
tor, "I wasn't thinking."

"What are you so nervous about?"

"Dunno. Jill's away and the maid's on holiday. I get a
bit tense when I'm on my own. I didn't know it showed."

I told her about the wipers. She nodded, changed down
for the next corner, forgot about the wipers and left them
on. An oncoming car flashed her to dip her lights. Ruth
bought a new car every year and always managed to bend
it. She held that she was careful but accident prone.

In the flat, she walked about, patting cushions, empty-
ing ash trays, examining records. "Nice place for pacing
up and down," I said, "a well-padded room."

"Pack it up," she said. "You know I don't like jokes about
padded rooms." She had had sessions with a psychiatrist

45

some years before. Malcolm had hinted that she was a hysteric. Personally I thought that psychiatry was one of Ruth's passing enthusiasms and that both the Flemings were too free in their use of the word "hysteric."

"I'm sorry," I began. "I'm a bit keyed up, too. I didn't mean . . ."

I looked at the door with its heavy, shining chromed lock. Lock?

"You didn't have a single lock in your last place," I said, "and now you even have a lock on the inside of your living-room door?"

"Yes, because there were no locks in the last place," she said.

"I don't think I follow you."

"You're not supposed to follow me."

"Come on, come on."

"You won't like it, but—okay. You know why there weren't any locks in the last house? Malcolm took them off, even the bathroom lock. When he was needling at me, needling at me, I used to go and lock myself *in*, oh, anywhere, anywhere to get away from his eyes and his voice. So he took the locks off the doors, even the lock off the bathroom door. I couldn't *keep* getting tradesmen to come and put locks on, it was too embarrassing. So we didn't have any locks. And every door locks here. Pretty sordid. Talk about something else?"

"Yes," I said.

"It's too damned silly," she said. "Let's have a drink." She poured two whiskies and two pint pots of beer, put her whisky back in one throw and began to sip the beer. When there were no other women present, she always drank like a man—like a plow hand, Malcolm said good-humoredly.

46

"Tell you what I'll do," she said, "I'll light that fire. This room's eerie without a fire." When the fire was lit, we sat on the sofa and watched it and gradually relaxed. She was right about the room, it needed a fire. It was carefully underfurnished with new, simple, modern pieces; very different from the living room of the house she had sold when Malcolm died. He had liked mellow things. He had often taken me to auction sales; searching for something which would help me share his enthusiasm; in much the way he had played record after record to me, until he found something which I liked. This was the way he helped me to appreciate good music.

"Do you still have Malcolm's records?" I asked.

"No, his father wanted them," she said. "I meant to replace them but I haven't got round to it yet. My records are a bit like this room, a bit brassy and modern. I think I'm getting over modern music and modern furniture. Want to hear a record?" I had to stop the grin. Ruth's enthusiasms were violent and fast in passing.

"No, thanks," I said, "I'm very happy sitting here with you, looking in the fire. So long as this lasts and the great, big ugly world is on the other side of those curtains, I've no problems and television never happened."

"Well, well, well," Ruth said. "After all those years. That's the first time you've ever made a pretty speech to me. You must try again sometime, when we've both got over the shock."

"No, I'll try again now. I think you're beautiful. I thought so the first day I met you. If you hadn't been Malcolm's wife, I would have clapped my Sam Browne belt round you and taken you to the moon."

"That's enough, that's fine," she said. "Don't say any more; you're beginning to spoil it. Anyway, whatever happened to that belt? I can remember it, it was so shiny."

"I gave it to a little boy to play pirates," I said. "He was called . . ." I trailed off, then, and took her hand. I had never held Ruth's hand before, except to help her out of a car, except when we were dancing. It was a strange sensation.

"It must be almost midnight," she said.

"Yes, I'd better go. You know what the night porter's like at the hotel."

"Yes, I know," she said. "I'll lift you back."

We stood up together, too quickly, too close. She laughed, uncertainly, and then I kissed her. "I don't think that's a very good idea," Ruth said. She put both hands behind my head and pulled it down and I kissed her nose and her mouth. We stumbled then and ended back on the couch.

"If you'll let me up, I'll get the car keys," she said.

"Don't bother," I said, "I'll walk. I'd rather walk." I moved her hair to kiss her neck, then she hit me hard on the shoulder with a clenched fist, three times.

"Don't," she said, "that's a very bad idea. I've been alone far too long for this. Don't." When I tried to kiss her again, she bit my lip. "We'd better be practical," she said. "You're in enough bother as it is. It's too much as if we're being driven into this. You'd better go. Oh, do that again. That's beautiful. Tom, for Christ's sake, go home."

"I will," I said, "I will."

A voice began a sermon in my head but when the sermon had gone on too long, a second voice began. *Why don't you belt up?* the second voice asked. *Go and haunt a Rechabite or something. Go and boil your can.* "How does this open?" I asked her.

48

"Say something nice," Ruth suddenly said. "Not later, not later. Say it now."

"Isn't it bloody marvelous to be alive?" Afterward, only half aware of talking, I also said, "I love you. I love you. I love you."

"No, you don't. But you will, you will."

We lay and watched the fire die.

"It's too late for you to go home now," Ruth said, at last. "We'll think of a story for you in the morning."

By lunchtime on the following day, we still hadn't thought of a story and I stayed on through the weekend. She was affectionate and warm; she made none of the usual brittle, edgy remarks; she looked very much as she had looked when I first met her. In the years between, I had often wondered if such a Ruth had existed only in my imagination.

When she said that she didn't gave a damn what people thought, she meant it. On Saturday, when the doorbell went, I was the one who panicked. It was an old lady collecting for a church restoration fund. She thanked me and my "wife" and said how nice it was nowadays to see young people looking happy.

It was the first time in my life I'd ever made love completely, easily and naturally. Before that, I'd thought that this was something which only the glib characters in the clinics thought was possible. I had none of the cold awareness of what was going on, none of the fear that it wouldn't end right. After the first evening, I didn't even have that first moment of embarrassment which I'd always known with Helen. Very rarely did I remember that I, Tom Cameron, was bunking up with her, Ruth Fleming. It struck me once when I was shaving; our toothbrushes in the same mug.

On Sunday we went walking in the woods early, before any others were about, not because we were afraid of meeting people, but because we wanted no company on the high track to the dam and the ruined castle beyond it which belongs to the nation and the crows.

All my life I'd known the woods. When Britain stood alone, I was commanding the Peewit Patrol of our scout troop and the hut in the wood had been our center while we did our bit, collecting wastepaper while the fly sheets for the tents gathered damp and the guy ropes went unspliced. For the first time in years, I didn't check that the hut was still there. Here I came with friends to plan our last Cairngorm holiday before we went our separate ways. That day I didn't spare them a thought.

Helen had known the woods when we first came home together. And once, in desert country, when the battalion was suffering from heat and a hold-up in the mail, from sand-fly fever and dysentery and boredom, Malcolm had talked about this wood and how it would be to walk there on an early autumn evening, in a light rain. I didn't remember that, until later. I didn't think of anything very much, I didn't talk, and neither did Ruth. Once, without saying anything, she pointed out a trick of light on beech leaves and once we kicked a stone ahead of us the length of a football pitch. Then we left it and walked on, so early and quiet in the woods that we came on the forester with his gun. He had a taste for venison and he was always on the lookout for deer loitering with intent in the neighborhood of forest nurseries. But on Sundays he normally vanished early. He could not stand the sight

50

of Sunday trippers who, when his back was turned, would try their strength on little trees. I knew him well; he waited for us at the top of a narrow track and Ruth asked me to go on ahead.

I think I must have blocked his view of her. "Hullo," he said, filling his pipe as a preliminary for talk. "You're not running away again, are you? Not with your wife right behind . . . Oh, I'm sorry. I beg your pardon. Good morning, Mrs. Fleming. Fine morning for a walk. The wireless says it'll hold good for the rest of the day. But I'll better not stand here, blethering. I have to get on." He forced the tobacco down, put the sliver pipe lid back in place, touched his cap awkwardly and walked off. At the opening of the track that led to his house, he turned and raised his hand to shoulder height, an abrupt farewell.

"What did he mean about running away?" Ruth asked.

"Oh, I ran away from school when I was seven or eight," I said, "and hid in the hut in the wood. After about twelve hours I was frightened to go home. When the forester found me, I asked him for a job."

"Eerie coincidence he should talk about running away," Ruth said.

"I've done all the running away I'm going to do," I said. "I'm with you and here I stay."

"No you won't," she said. "Every time this happens, you'll think of Helen and Malcolm. You'll run away again when it happens often enough. I wish you could see your face."

I tried to persuade her that it wasn't so; then we walked in a different quiet to the end of the wood and the high dyke, where the forester leaves skinned vermin hanging like bats, in warning. Beyond it was a shapeless hill, with-

51

out a tree, and the track which was corrugated with rain and carts and sun. As she walked, she whipped the heads from weeds with a piece of ash, deliberately.

We picnicked by the lochan, which was a secret sea when I was small and which shrinks with every visit. I had written about it once for the My Home section of an Army wall sheet which we kept on the troop deck of a ship, pasting up our thought pieces with condensed milk. I didn't like the way my thoughts kept drifting back to my also-served war; this had been happening ever since the night of the *première*. I drove it out and looked at Ruth, who was lying in the heather, chewing at a bit of grass, with my jacket under her head.

"The first time I ever saw you was here," I said. "You were wearing a sweater, and you were the only girl without a ribbon in your hair. You were with a lot of characters in their first set of longs, very okay accents and shining bikes with three-speed gears. You gave one of them a hammering, over there, beside the boathouse."

"I remember, too," she said. "I had to do something. I was trying to impress you." This seemed such an outrageous lie that I ignored it and lashed out at a wandered wasp.

"All right, don't believe me," she said. "You were with a couple of other boys, you were all wearing rucksacks with blankets on the outside and billycans hanging on the straps. You were about five miles beyond the bus terminus and you looked like you'd just tackled Kanchenjunga. After that, I got keen on hill walking . . . for a while."

I laughed. "I'll bet you did," I said, "and surf riding . . . for a while, and skiing . . . for a while. And when you were

52

keen on hill walking, you would know all there was to know, to the pony tracks on Loch Ailort. And you would be really caught up in the history of it all. I'll bet you could even quote the English law against the wearing of the kilt."

When she was angry, faint arrowheads of lines showed at the corners of her mouth. "Don't be so damned patronizing," she said. "What do you mean?"

"You're like that. You have these wonderful white enthusiasms for hobbies and ideas and jobs . . . and people. You wave them around like sparklers and don't worry too much when they die. I like it; I never know what's going to happen next. But I don't want to be a sparkler. Let me be the lighter; a good solid table model. Let me watch."

She threw a tin from the picnic basket at me then. When I threw it back at her, as hard, she forgot her injured dignity and laughed.

"The little kids used to shout, 'Gray breeks, gray breeks, let's hear you speaking pan-loafy,'" she said.

I concentrated on a ripple in the water. When I was small I had shouted that, too. An all-girls school where they paid fees and wore gray uniforms and didn't talk in the local accent was splendidly ridiculous.

"It made me lonely, you know?" Ruth said. "I didn't have a father or a brother or a sister and I didn't get on with the other girls in my class."

"No?" When she talked about her school days or her youth, she was worried about something. The way she worked things out, her school days, her youth, her mother, were the source of all her troubles.

"And the boys," she said. "'Three-speed gears and very okay accents.' They were nice boys but dull. I envied you.

I wanted to go up to the hills like your girl friend did, later, the daft girl with fair hair. What was her name?"

"Rhoda, Rhoda Ogilvie." Rhoda was married to an important man in Local Government now and very respectable. Her daughter studied ballet and her small son was kept at the piano and briefed on the youth of Mozart.

"You were all so free," Ruth said. "Not me. I brought a girl home once, a nice girl. When she went away, Mother kept talking about the way she spread jam with the spoon from the jam dish."

"Oh, we were burdened with the class struggle, too," I said. At the high school, most of the boys were from the homes of tradesmen or shopkeepers and they made it hard for us, the 'scholars.' Some 'scholars' would pretend to be better off, so that they could enter the aristocracy of grocers' sons, but there was usually something to give them away; the clothes they had at weekends when school blazers were not worn, the cheap soccer shorts their mothers bought them to play rugby; the home address with the grandiloquent street name of a council housing estate. One bright girl in our physics class left school when the other girls found out that she lived in a tenement with a common lavatory on the stairs.

"But it was better later on, wasn't it?" Ruth persisted. "When you got to be sixteen or seventeen?"

She was partly right. When we left school, the hard patterns of class began to fade a little. I'd met some of the worst snobs in London since and had been impressed by the fictitious working-class backgrounds they'd acquired. By then, they were caught up in the general belief that a lower-middle-class upbringing was something to be ashamed of, while to have risen from the working class

54

was noble, a source of righteous anger. They were suddenly comradely. . . .

"Well, it wasn't for me." She talked about the boys she knew who joined the Forces. "They used to come round like courting Victorians," she said, "and sometimes take me to the Rep to see *Dear Octopus* for a basinful of culture. They used to say things like 'It's not on, old girl' and 'a chap in the regiment.' Awful imitation English accents. I wanted to cover my legs with sun-tan lotion and draw lines down the back, as if I was wearing stockings. And dance in the Palais to 'Silver Wings in the Moonlight' with R.A.F. ground crew. I'd rather have been tarty than lonely. You knew the Palais?"

"I was educated at the Palais," I said. It hadn't struck me before that our town was too small and the rich too few for their young to have anything but a meager separate society. "No boy friends?" I asked. "No exotic boy friends?"

"There was one," she said, "a Canadian pilot. I ran away with him but it didn't work out. In the hotels, I had to hide my ration book . . . it was one of those special ones for people under sixteen and still entitled to a ration of bananas. He kept joking about that. I went home."

I knew where this was leading now. "Then Malcolm turned up," I said, "and your mother liked him and when you were old enough you had one of these wartime marriages that were never any good."

She began to pack the basket. "The man-of-the-world act doesn't suit you," she said. "Let's go."

When I looked for a pencil that evening, Ruth suggested that I get one from the top drawer of Jill's cupboard. I went into the fitted wardrobe by mistake and looked for long enough at her first school uniform . . . the tiny pleated skirt, the blazer with its freshly minted badge, the badge of Ruth's school, for her the badge of "loneliness." In the room with its circus wallpaper, soft furry toys and transfers on the white wood door, this looked like another dressing-up set, like the nurse's cap and cape.

Then I found the right cupboard and the right drawer. There were no pencils in the pencil box or under the tin of paints, among the tangle of wool and beads and dolls' arms. There was a small imitation suitcase made of papier mâché and I opened it, in hope. It held a "doctor's set" in plastic, some lint, a pair of scissors, a pencil and Malcolm's watch strap.

I put it all back, quickly, including the pencil—I had been scavenging in private places. I remembered Malcolm on the last few times I'd seen him, when he'd changed, when he didn't snap out of his depression so easily, when he thought that he was losing touch with Jill as well as Ruth.

He once told me about taking her for a walk, after he'd had a row with Ruth, when Jill was well aware of it but, as always, pretending that she had not heard a thing. The walk had gone all right until he kicked her ball into a tree. Jill wouldn't believe him at first when he said he couldn't get it down. Then she had made a scene and insisted on going home. This was the day she found out that her father wasn't God.

"Find it?" Ruth asked, when I went back to the living room.

"No, but it's all right, I've found my pen." She was reading about the stars, which was her latest enthusiasm. She'd found out that a star burst had been observed a year or two before, that the star was one and a half times the size of the sun, which, she'd also found out, was as much larger than the earth as a football is larger than a speck of dust.

I couldn't get caught up in her enthusiasm. I kept thinking of something much smaller than an exploding star. I was thinking of a sparkler.

That night I couldn't get to sleep. I kept wondering at what stage in their marriage Malcolm's sparkler had gone out.

I kept checking on the time. This is essential in judging how few are the hours of sleep and how tired you should feel in the morning. It was after three when Ruth stirred and cried. It took some minutes to draw her from the dream.

"The last time we were close," she said, "you went away and left a thank-you note and I didn't see you for years."

"That was different. I had to do that. I don't have to do that now. I love you."

"You don't have to say that. Say it when you mean it, when you really mean it." Her flat was on the top floor and rain was hissing on the roof, masquerading the sound of silence. "Nice to lie in bed and listen to rain," she said, and went on talking, the voice growing slow, as she expressed thoughts drifting through her head. Rain at night made her think of her father. Before he went away, she was sometimes allowed to sleep in summer in a tent in the garden. When the rain fell, he would come out and check on her and put the blankets to his mouth to check for damp. If it was dry inside, he would let her stay. Rain, too, meant the bothy that she owned, not far from Arisaig. When it came in summer, on the southwest wind from

57

the sea, and hammered on the window, she wasn't worried. There would always be that moment when it cleared, when the light broke through, when the blues and greens of the sea, the purple and green and sand of the land were fantastic, unlike anything elsewhere in the world. Maybe I thought it was strange that she should talk of loneliness and own a bothy in South Morar. But it wasn't all that strange. If you couldn't rid yourself of loneliness, it was better to face up to it. They knew how to deal with loneliness there; they didn't huddle together in fear of it or go on talking to fill the empty air like sheep, she said.

This was the best time to be with a woman, when she lay talking in the night. This was the best reason for making love to a woman, to find what she was all about. The preachers knew nothing of this, of the tough, temporary bridges thrown across the gap between two lonely people. . . .

"You were going to the Highlands, weren't you?" she asked.

"I *was* going, but—"

"No buts. No buts. Where did you want to go?"

"Oh, dunno. Lots of places but I didn't bring the car." I'd left the car at the garage nearest Helen's sister's place and asked her to collect it. Helen had ignored it. The car wasn't used to cover. By now it would be suffering from screaming claustrophobia.

"That's easy enough if you let me come," Ruth said, "if you want me to come. Are you sure? I'll ask you again in the morning. We could go to this bothy of mine for a bit, if you like. It would be nice having a man there. Malcolm always used to make up reasons why he couldn't come. He didn't like me having bits of property."

58

This was unreasonable of her. She was rich, Malcolm had not been. He had not liked working in his father's business. Ruth's money had only made the job more trivial. He was bound to be sensitive about her property. "Honey," I said, "I don't think we should talk about Malcolm right now." Things would go wrong the moment we started having cozy chats about Malcolm or Helen. "The way you asked me about Malcolm's last patrol, the other night. I know nothing about it. For a while, anyway, we don't want to talk about Malcolm."

"You don't think I was asking you for fun?" she said. "You don't think I was making light conversation? It was very funny, you know, you were in the battalion and you never heard about that patrol . . . nothing good about it, nothing bad. I'm beginning to wonder if the film company's right."

I sat up and put the bed light on. I had been trying not to think about the film, trying to deal with one trouble at a time. "What's this about the film company?"

She was blinking and I turned the bed light upward. "I'll tell you some other time," she said. "In the morning, if you like."

"Why not now?"

"In the morning."

"Why not now?"

She got out of bed. "All right," she said, "I'll make some coffee; you might need it." She draped my dressing gown over her shoulders and led the way to the kitchen.

"Big trouble from the film company," she said, as she set out cups on a tray. "They're in a stushy. Some of the survivors started creating hell about the film, right after the *première*. They're threatening to tell the papers or

59

even take it to court. They're saying that Malcolm was a coward on that last patrol and that it was his fault that Ramsay and the others got killed."

At the best of times there's a lack of reality about a kitchen, trembling with neon at three in the morning, when it's black outside, when familiar things like cups seem to change their color and their shape. I couldn't take this in.

"That's poppycock," I said. "Macphail was talking like that at the *première*. Must be a few soreheads like him who reckon that they should have made a fortune from the film or won fame overnight, or some damned thing. Malcolm tried to save Ramsay."

"What did Macphail say?"

"Oh, nothing much. He hinted at something like this. War heroes are always so tedious and vain in peacetime. That was one of the reasons Malcolm never talked about the war. He was different."

"I hope he wasn't too different," Ruth said. "The film company are going to start an investigation, so they can defend themselves if the whole thing blows up."

"What do they mean by an 'investigation'? Private detectives calling on Malcolm's parents to see his papers, interviewing survivors, sniffing round the regimental depot and so on?"

"Something like that. I've been trying not to think about it, trying not to bother you about it. I don't think there's a thing that we can do," she said.

"When do they start in?"

She had the impression that the film company wouldn't begin for at least a month, to give them just enough time to get the facts before the film went out on circuit. This

60

made sense; the film was ending in the West End and it would have to wait for a circuit booking; there was the normal press of war films waiting to be shown. The film company would not move until they were forced, when indignant heroes went to their local papers.

"Why did he let them make the film?" I asked.

"I don't know," she said, "I don't know. He was a bit odd before the end. I think he thought he was cheated, or something like that."

"Maybe he was cheated," I said, "and maybe in a different way he's being cheated now. Whatever else, we can't have the private detective stuff. Even when they clear him, they'll leave a smell."

"What can I do?" she asked. "I said I didn't know about the patrol and the film company wanted to know if I could find out. But what chance have I got? The regiment, Macphail and the others, they'd never give *me* all the facts; they'd never give me a chance to get it straight."

The coffee burned my mouth. I wasn't too worried about heroism as it is understood in war films. But an attempt to brand Malcolm as a liar and a fraud was different.

"They might tell me," I said. "It's maybe just as well we're going north. I'll start off before you."

6

The train north was slow on the hills, having left England, the Scottish Lowlands and the people who spent the day regretting the lost moments of the day before.

On my way to the regimental depot, I had plenty of time to think about the patrol. When I'd told Ruth that Malcolm had said nothing about the patrol, I hadn't been entirely truthful. From time to time when I asked him direct questions about the patrol, he had given me answers which had seemed witty, sophisticated, wise. Now, I had to admit, they seemed glib, oblique.

The patrol had come about when the Karens in the mountains in the southeast of Burma were about to rise. We were parachuting in arms and needed men to follow the arms to train the Karens to use them and to remind them that they were not alone.

The Karens had old associations with the regiment from the wars against the Burmese in the nineteenth century. It was decided that one of the patrols should come entirely from our regiment, for tradition's sake. But they had to be men who had already proved themselves on missions and officers and N.C.O.'s of the regiment were drawn in from all the corners of Special Service.

Fleming and Macphail came from Special Boat Section, Lieutenant Ramsay from Special Force 136, the doctor, Drummond, who had once served with the regiment, from a Commando on the Arakan, others from further afield.

This movement had fascinated me but Malcolm said that it was only another illustration of how the brass hats liked to shift men from station to station. He said that the brass hats were all train spotters in their secret hearts. I argued that the Karens at least would appreciate it and he said, yes, indeed they did. He added that when "the English ruled the world with a velvet hand in an iron glove," they showed little understanding of us Scots. They showed no mercy in any century to the Irish and their idea of diplomacy in India was to flag march through Amritsar with bayonets fixed. But they knew the Karens, Christian savages like themselves, with a similar taste for melodrama, he said.

If he answered about the patrol at all, he always talked like that. Once, someone in the mess asked him about the plane they used, when they parachuted into Burma. It would be a special plane? For an important assignment, the beginning of the Karen rebellion, perhaps the bloodiest rebellion anywhere in the whole of the war?

Oh, it was special all right, Malcolm had said. They got the worst pilot and the worst navigator in the whole of the long-range reconnaissance squadrons. It was a great joke among the aircraft's crew that the navigator always carried his correspondence course on bookkeeping on every flight, against the day when he would be shot down, so that he could finish his course in a prison camp. Also they swore that the pilot was worse, that when once he was attacked by a Zero, he kept on flying his plane on the automatic pilot.

Malcolm didn't see the joke himself, particularly when this "pair of comics" managed to drop them four or five days' march from the place they were supposed to reach. No doubt they took quiet pride in the fact that they found the right river, Malcolm said, and dropped them somewhere on the Irrawaddy rather than the Salween or the Clyde or something of the kind. He had heard that a stick of parachutists, intended for the North African campaign, were dropped in Spain.

He admitted that they had good supply drops—and reminded the questioner that, at that stage of the war, there were other considerations in Burma besides fighting the Japanese. We had to give the Burmese medicine and food, he said, to remind them that if the English were not the best possible tenants Burma could have, they were "gentlemen at least and they always paid the rent."

In the train, I realized that Malcolm had done a fair amount of talking about the patrol, but in answering questions, he had avoided saying anything significant. His answers didn't seem as brilliant as they once had but I supposed he had been awkward, hiding his true feelings about the patrol by being facetious. Facetious, that was the word. . . . not oblique, not devious. Film companies panic easily. War veterans are most belligerent in defense of their inaccurate memories of old campaigns.

It would be simple, an hour or two with the records at the depot would clear it up. I was glad Ruth hadn't kept it to herself any longer.

At first I had seen Malcolm in too glorious a light but, as I grew older and got to know him and the light mellowed, I still admired him. He could never have done this thing.

A sergeant of the regiment came into the carriage at the last station before the depot, and we started talking. He complained about the discipline at the depot, he said that there were still too many old men about, remembering what it was like in the Great War, out of touch with the way that he'd had to fight. I agreed with him, thinking that he was talking of Ypres and the Somme. It turned out that he was comparing Korea and the Second World War.

"Who's commanding the depot now?" I asked, to change the subject.

"Colonel Humphries," he said.

"Oh, no," I said, "he can't still be here."

"Oh, aye," the sergeant said grimly, "oh, aye. He's still here, he never fades away. You know him, then?"

"I know him," I said. I should also have known that Colonel Humphries would hang on for all the years he could and that the right place for him was the regimental depot, where he could instil regimental pride into young soldiers until they shone like boots. Malcolm and Humphries had never got on. I hoped Colonel Humphries had an obliging adjutant.

"If you know him, you'll know what to expect," the sergeant said, "so much haggis-bashing and Highland tradition that we're expecting him to recall the king frae o'er the watter and march on London, any day. If he had his way, we'd be opening bully-beef tins with basket-handled claymores, and he would *make* us eat salt porridge if he could. The other night there, a man was asking me if I thought that Colonel Humphries had heard of the Bomb."

"He has," I said. At the end of the war Colonel Humphries was a major in temporary command of our battalion. After the news from Hiroshima and Nagasaki he ordered all subalterns to write an essay on *The Future of Highland Infantry in the Light of the Atom Bomb*. Colonel Humphries was an Englishman from an old Devon family, but his heart was always in the Highlands. We discussed that, then the sergeant asked my name.

"Cameron," he repeated; "you should have been in the Camerons instead of us, with that name. But if I had a Highland name, any Highland name, there would be no holding me in this battalion. Is it my fault I'm a Scot with the name of Jones? There's still one English sergeant in the depot and he has no chance at all. Colonel Humphries

65

fairly persecutes him. The old story, eh? They say that the guards with Jewish blood were always the biggest bastards in the concentration camps. But I'll say this for him. The regiment's been twice the regiment since he took over here. This is where we get off. This is where I have to be twice the man."

The regimental depot was as grim and black as I remembered it. Our regiment is the most junior of Highland infantry, younger even than the Argylls, but the post-war recruiting figures had been good. When other regiments, including the Camerons and Seaforths, were amalgamated, ours remained intact. It had not survived because of its beautiful home.

I'd undergone recruit training here and the influence of the place was still so strong that I hesitated as my left foot crossed the saluting sticks, placed at twenty paces round the guard room. The old barbarous custom of having a mirror on the guardroom floor had been revived. By this, guard commanders could make sure that a recruit did not wear swimming trunks under his kilt when he walked out. The rules were stern. Officers and men could only wear shorts trews or have their shirttails pinned together, if they were taking part in Highland dancing.

I told the corporal of police that I had to see the adjutant.

"Just a minute, sir, I'll send an escort with you," he said, then stiffened, took a pace to the rear, swung round while his kilt moved like the wings of a landing duck, halted. *"One man!"* he screamed. In our regiment, all words of command are given at the scream. Malcolm used to say that this helped to make the prevailing lunacy seem normal.

66

On the way to the orderly room, we passed three glowering barrack blocks, each named after a battle in which the regiment had won honor. In the old days, we had all taught regimental history to those whom Colonel Humphries called the Jocks, although the battalion was heavily depleted after its campaigning and the "Jocks" were eighty per cent English, drawn from all the regiments of the Highland Brigade. We were forced to preface our remarks with, "Regimental history. All men originally from the Black Watch, Gordons, Camerons, Seaforths or Argylls—outside." New English recruits had looked sad and thoughtful at that moment.

If Malcolm *had* chosen a new legend for the regiment he would not have been the first. According to the "history" we taught, the regiment had never been responsible for a defeat and the men had never behaved in any fashion short of the heroic. But our regimental "history" was inclined to clash with the "history" of the other Highland regiments and interregimental rivalry is very fierce in the Highland Brigade. When the Black Watch and the Argylls were together in Perth in wartime, their closing-hour bus-stop fights were so regular and so fierce that bus conductresses automatically shouted, "Black Watch to the front, Argylls to the rear." We knew of every disgrace ever suffered by our sister regiments. When the war ended, according to us, each German soldier was ordered to hand over his rifle and one Gordon Highlander.

The escort left me at the orderly room and I stood looking beyond the clerks for the colonel's door. I had no desire to bump into Humphries. There was an officer wearing civilian clothes in the orderly room, a much younger man than Humphries. He turned and we recognized each other at the same time.

"Well, well," he said, "Tom Cameron. Yourself, is it? And several sizes larger than life as usual." Fergus Macdonald had a wonderfully stilted Highland voice. It was often said in the mess that Fergus was a terrible snob, that he hadn't spoken in that affected Highland way at Eton. He was an old friend and we shook hands warmly. "You're not offering to come back, are you now?" Fergus asked. "Not to your taste, at all. There would be no hope for you here, dancing the foursome like a sack of spuds the way you do."

"Shush, the adjutant will hear you."

"Quite likely," Macdonald said, "since I'm the adjutant, myself. Come into my office and sit yourself down and give us your patter. What can I do for you?" I told him when his door was closed and I was surprised by his reaction.

"The film," Fergus said. "Aye, we heard about it and we've been expecting trouble. The best way to be a hero is to make up a fairy story about yourself and have it filmed. And that's the truth from that moment. That's what the public believe. Nothing that anyone ever says will ever alter it."

"Would you mind explaining?" In the old days, Fergus had been a rebel and as great an admirer of Malcolm as I was.

"Not I, not I. That's not talked about in the regiment and you'll never hear about it from me. Nobody talked about it in the old days. Use your head. We thought there would be trouble about that film and the colonel's orders are that no one will say anything to anyone. Can't even

68

give you the addresses. I'm sorry, Tom, I'm sorry. You'd better come and have tea."

On the path to the mess his good spirits revived. As we passed a relief map of the area, he reminded me of the time we were sent on a map-reading course together, when the adjutant had told us that our ignorance of map reading suggested simple-mindedness, that the sickroom attendants had been exposed to more elements than we had and that the Wrens were better jungle fighters.

"Remember?" he asked. "When we took out C Company and all those merry jesters at the back looked at our maps and compasses and asked when the vultures would start to follow us? Was it McGregor who said that we were the gravest error the Army had made since the fall of Singapore?"

"It was McNally, Ramsay's old batman. They say that Malcolm was responsible for Ramsay's death."

Fergus gripped my shoulder. "Will you drop it?" he said. "Will you drop it? Some good men were killed there and the patrol achieved its purpose. The thing's finished. Fleming wasn't court-martialed. He's dead and that's that. . . . Good afternoon, Corporal." He had stopped to acknowledge a salute.

"There was that time in jungle training camp," I said, "when we were told to make a raft of female bamboo, for male bamboo didn't float too well." I had not given up hope.

"And the raft sank under us?" Fergus said. "I'm convinced to this day that it was female bamboo. You and I never had any luck with women."

His next words were drowned by a piper playing "A Man's a Man For a' That," to summon defaulters to clean out the latrines. This was a grand old Highland Brigade joke, untarnished by the passing of time. I wanted to hear a wilder pipe rant.

In the mess, Colonel Humphries was having tea and Fergus waited until the colonel had spread his jam before we walked across.

"Scrimgeour Cameron," the colonel said. "No need to introduce him. Sit down, sit down."

It was fitting that he should remember my proper Christian name. People who don't actively dislike me tend to forget it. The colonel looked bewildered rather than distressed, as he considered my clothes. It was customary in the regiment for officers officially in civilian clothes to wear a suit of the regimental tweed, a grey shirt from the regimental tailor and a regimental tie.

"As individual as ever, eh?" the colonel asked. "And what sort of—uhummph—job are you doing in civilian life?" I told him and he seemed interested. In the whole of my Army career, I had never made a remark which had interested Colonel Humphries.

"Television, eh?" the colonel said. "And you're not an electronic engineer or anything like that? Or trained for senior command? How did you manage it? Which—ah—group are you with?"

"Commercial, sir." I imagined that, if the colonel had progressed beyond the original social game of view and nonview, he would have stuck with the B.B.C., the regular forces. He would feel that the B.B.C. news gave the people the right sort of news, the news that would not alarm them.

But I was wrong. The colonel was with the intellectuals who looked down on the B.B.C. from the dreaming spires

70

of their polytechnics. He was a cowboys-and-Indians snob. The colonel couldn't stand the pretensions of the B.B.C. and their so-called documentary program. But he had to admit, he had to admit, Cameron, that he had never missed the best of the cowboy things, especially that big good-natured fellow. His tune goes something like this. . . .

"I've been wondering, Cameron," the colonel said, "I've been wondering how television can help us in the infantry. One must keep up with the times, you know. I suppose . . . sooner or later, there will be television signaling sets that a man or, let's say, a jeep could carry? Color television, for directing artillery support and that sort of thing?"

I told him there were many ex-Service signals people *in* television and that I expected they would be thinking along those lines. So far as I knew the ex-Service signals people were heavily occupied in trying to run television companies as if they were armored regiments or aircraft carriers, but this would have been an undiplomatic thing to say.

"Really? How interesting, very," the colonel said. Apart from the military possibilities of television, he felt that we shouldn't forget the power of publicity today. If I ever wanted to do a program on the regiment, I could easily arrange it through Scottish Command. "Some good publicity for the regiment might balance up for that film, don't you think? I heard they had a police pipe band at the *première*. A *police* pipe band!"

"The film about Malcolm Fleming, sir?"

"The film which was supposed to be about Fleming," the colonel said. He looked at his watch to indicate that the subject was closed and Fergus warned me to shut up, as he had always warned me, by a hard kick with a heavy brogue.

When the colonel had gone, a buzz of talk began and one bold youngster lit a pipe, something he would never have dared to do at table in Colonel Humphries' presence. In our regiment, pipes may be smoked on the march, after the second halt of the day. Like everything else, pipes have their proper place.

Fergus tapped on the table. "Fraser," he said, "put that bloody thing out. Smoke-screen canisters are being standardized throughout NATO ground forces." He spoke with quiet authority; he'd always had the makings of a regimental soldier. The subaltern rose, apologized and left the table. Then Fergus asked me to come up to his room while he changed. Soon he would have to inspect a barrack room with Humphries and I could imagine that barrack room, with blankets barracked in harmonious, multicolored blocks like layer cake, mess tins flanking water bottles and blancoed gaiters at the open order, heady with the smell of Blanco Number 103, Khaki Green.

Fergus had the normal cell of an officer living without his wife; furnished in anonymity apart from prints and books and photographs. There was a photograph of his daughter on a pony and I wondered if every Army officer with a daughter had a photograph of her on a pony. He put on his tunic.

"Fergus, for Christ's sake. Congratulations. Where did you get the Military Cross?"

He buttoned the tunic slowly and didn't answer for a minute. "The only place you get it nowadays," he said. "In a police action as you call it. A stupid, half-paid soldier fighting for the bloated capitalists and the empire on which the sun never rises. While all you clever civilians sit back and laugh at us. I got it in Malaya, as a matter of fact, defending rubber shares and annoying the weekly reviews. Tom, you're sitting on my gaiters."

I moved. "Wait, now wait," I said, "what's this all about?" I couldn't see his face; he was taking a spot of brass polish from his belt.

"I was listening to you with Humphries," he said, "listening to you having a quiet laugh at a silly soldier who'd just heard about television."

I handed him a cloth to remove the polish and I said that I didn't follow him, that I hadn't said much to Humphries. "No, you said a little and you assumed he was too stupid to follow your thought," Fergus said. "Well, he's not, you know. It would have done you no harm to try to interest him as he was trying to interest you."

He was right; my one defense was in anger, in attack, in saying that Humphries hadn't changed enough to interest me, that he was still the all-for-it bastard who'd made our life a misery. "That sort of talk was all very well when you and I were a pair of pimply-faced James Deans before it was the fashion," Fergus said. "But it's different now; I thought you would see that. It's not for you and me to argue whether this country needs Highland infantry or not. But if we're going to have it, we might as well have it good. A man is better off when he's proud of himself and his regiment." He examined his tam-o'-shanter. "Especially," he said, "especially when every smart character in journalism or television who ever did jankers in wartime is anxious to laugh at us, to say what fools we are for staying on, to show that recruiting's only

73

stimulated by bed lamps and red jackets and four-course cookhouse meals; to remind us that we're as out of date as pikes. When you have these jokers on you, you need men like Colonel Humphries."

I would have given a lot to have had that afternoon over again, never to have let Fergus guess how I felt about the infantry; especially now when he grew ashamed of his outburst and began to complain about his batman who, he said, was the heavy lead of the Sick Parade.

"You've got it wrong," I said. "I wasn't talking to Humphries as the colonel-in-charge of the depot. I was talking to him as the man who always had a down on Malcolm. You ought to remember that. It wasn't all 'James Dean before it was the fashion.' Remember the day we heard the atom bomb was dropped? Remember Humphries had us writing essays and it was left to Malcolm to explain it properly to us, to let us think straight? It was Malcolm who talked about the bomb that day the way so many thinking men are talking now."

Fergus had finished dressing and he sat down on the edge of a chair, taking care not to mark his belt. "I don't have to remember," he said. "I've thought about it often and I'm thinking now that you're fooling yourself. Malcolm did *not* say what thinking men are saying now. He said that the bomb was more of a warning to the Russians, an attempt to intimidate them, than it was a way of ending with Japan. That was a very impressive argument for a pair of kids like us. The main thing about Fleming was that he wasn't so much clever as mentally glib. He had a very twisted view of things, for all his gaiety, and he was damned good at putting his view across when he had a few chosen pupils at his feet. It wasn't deliberate, mind.

74

He made the same mistake about himself as we made, listening to him. He mistook clarity of expression for logic. And if that mouthful of words doesn't convince you that I've thought about this, what will?"

Beneath his window, the regimental sergeant major was crossing the drill square toward the mess to join Fergus. Time was short. I said there was one thing Fergus had forgotten. He had forgotten how little time they had for me in the 1st Battalion because I wasn't like them and how little time they had for Fergus because he was a renegade. It was Fleming who looked after us.

He laughed then. "You think that, do you? When you had a chip a mile high and you were always looking for characters with fancy accents to knock it off, majors and above for preference? I won't go into my own troubles now, but has it never struck you that this was a funny attitude for the like and age of Fleming to be encouraging in us? And we weren't half as unpopular as we tried to be. Did you ever see what was written about you in the regimental magazine, when you left the battalion?"

I had. I wouldn't have expected a better testimonial from my Mum. It must have been a mistake.

"Mistake," he said. "Aye, Fleming didn't teach you to think straight, he taught you to think squint. Humphries wrote that bit about you and it was no mistake. Come on, we'll have to go." He asked me to write my address and phone number in his book. He said that he would call on me in London, that he sometimes felt an "awful need for argument." When I was writing, I asked him where I would find Sergeant Major Sampson. The sergeant on the train had told me Sampson was at the depot.

"I was waiting for that," Fergus said. "I was wondering

when that would come up. You were always a great man for a lost cause. Lost Cause Cameron. You'll find Sampson on the bayonet range at this very moment. He'll tell you nothing about Fleming that will do you any good. I ought to send you out through the gates, under escort. But, on you go and for God's sake go out through the kitchen and dodge the colonel. On you go, on you go."

On the range, the recruits stood by the sawdust-filled bayonet targets. They had no shirts, the sweat was running free, some tam-o'-shanters were falling over eyes, others clinging to the backs of scalps. The tam-o'-shanters were of the regulation enormity, known in the regiment as cow dung or landing strips. Men were not allowed to have their tam-o'-shanters cut to a reasonable size until they were trained.

"On *guard!*" Sergeant Major Sampson screamed and the rifles came up and the bayonets gleamed in the sun. "As you were," the sergeant major said. "Move in double time. A skilled bayonet fighter must have determination to *kill.*" I'd known him as a young, unruly N.C.O. He had been on Malcolm's last patrol.

"First lot," the sergeant major said. "I heard you, Private Grant. You didn't learn that language in this regiment. First lot, and look lively. Lot of nig-nogs off the trees. I've a good mind to write to my M.P. about you lot. Right. At the dummy. Point. You, Moral Danger there, shouldn't ought to have been mustered. Scream when you stick your bayonet in."

"Aauh," the recruit said.

"*Scream!*"

"AAAUUUH!"

"*Scream!*"

"Aaeeeeeeeh!"

"And again. Too much fat on you, a swill bin, crazed with wolfing marzipan again. Stop that man over there, Corporal. Give that Teddy King a special sawdust dummy of his own. Running amok. Turned savage at the sight of sawdust. Next file. At the dummy, *point*. As you were. Take over, Corporal. Bunch of nig-nogs off the trees. Good afternoon, Mr. Cameron. Don't tell me you're in need of bayonet practice?"

He walked across on his heels, with his head held high, with all the swagger of a parade-ground sergeant major, but he was smiling. Twice I'd got him out of trouble in the battalion.

"Good afternoon," I said. "You've changed. You swore you would never stay in."

"It was either that or running guns," he said, "and there's a better pension in the Army."

"Do the recruits know that you were in the last bayonet charge of the regiment?"

"*Bayonet* charge!" he said. "*Bayonet* charge! I heard about that. That was in the picture, wasn't it? Mr. Cameron, we never had a dog's chance to use the bayonet," he said with deep regret. "We were saved by young Ramsay and a Bren gun."

"Wasn't it Major Fleming with the Bren gun?"

"Major Fleming be knackered. It was Ramsay. They're both dead but I can tell you it was Ramsay. And why are you asking? My name's Sampson and I'm from Kelty and Kelty's the center of Scotland and there are no flies on me. Why are you asking, at this stage of the game?" I had forgotten that he was proud of his local custom of answer-

ing my question with another. I told him why, in detail.
I could trust him. "I can't tell you. I've had a direct order
from the colonel. I can't," he said.

"Dougal Macphail told me something."

"Then let him tell you the rest, if you have to know.
He'll not exaggerate it. He's out of the Army and up on
the island of Inish. And don't tell anybody I said a word
to you about it."

Macphail was prejudiced against Malcolm. If I heard
his story, I wanted to hear one that balanced it off and I
asked Sampson if there was any man who had gone
through the whole patrol and stayed on Fleming's side.

"There was one man," Sampson said, "only one. Young
Cochrane, a damned good soldier. But you'll have a bit of
trouble reaching him. He was a bit of a lone dog after
that patrol, always arguing on Fleming's side, and he had
too much to drink on his own on V-J Day. He was leaning
over a basin when he drowned in his own puke." Sampson stopped and looked round. "Quick," he said to me,
"get out of sight. Parade, PARADE, 'SHUN!" Colonel Humphries was walking past with his eyes on the ground.
Fergus Macdonald walked behind him and pretended not
to notice as I dodged behind the weapon store.

A hearse went by as I left the depot. It was empty, but
I stood watching it until it reached the corner. At the best
of times I never see a hearse or pass a cemetery without
reacting badly. I once read that the Spaniards were a mature people who gave calm and contemplative thought to
death as a mature people should and that this partly explained their interest in bullfighting, particularly in the
last moments of the bull. I was impressed by that and I
watched several bullfights, hoping that the calm and

contemplative mood would come on soon, but I saw the last moments of too many glorious bulls, stabbed and sapped by the picadors, carrying three darts and two swords, standing or staggering, pouring blood; wondering which of the golden pygmies it should charge. This was not tragedy. This was funereal farce.

I've gone to considerable trouble never to see a dead man. I've dreamed of lying in a graveyard, with my headstone behind me and my feet sticking out into the path, so that visitors to other graves tripped over them. When the hearse was out of sight, I wondered how I would have reacted in Malcolm Fleming's place, on that last patrol, with the fear of death on me.

Then I rang Ruth and told her what I'd found out. I didn't believe that things could be as black as Fergus and Hector Sampson had suggested. It would certainly take longer to find out what had happened. For a start I would have to go straight to Macphail. The Inish mailboat sailed from Mallaig on Saturday mornings.

"I'll be back on Saturday night," I promised her. "I'll see you in your cottage. Macphail's story can't be worse than all the rumors. Malcolm might have had just one bad spell, maybe just one day when he couldn't cope with things, when he was suddenly frightened."

"Suddenly frightened?" she said. "But he was used to it. He'd got over it—what do you call it—his baptism of fire?"

"Let's leave it until we get more details," I said. A woman as nervous as Ruth might have understood what Malcolm had gone through.

"Yes. Did you know you left your raincoat? Remember to buy a plastic mac or something."

7

By eleven the following morning I was in Mallaig, at the end of the Road to the Isles. I walked the last few hundred yards of the Road for they were owned by British Railways, ending in a huddle of huts where the fish-gutting girls lived. This extremity of the Road was locally known as Chinatown and you'd never smell the tangle of the isles there. The smell and smoke of kipper curing was stronger. But I liked Mallaig; it satisfied the honest lust for authenticity that all tourists experience in a fishing port.

A fisherman was repairing nets on the jetty. "That's hard work," I said.

"Aye, but you can't expect fish just to jump into the boat, now can you?" he asked.

"Have you seen any signs of the Inish mail boat?"

"The Inish mail boat?" the fisherman repeated, then he laughed. He was an East Coast Scot, Buchan by his accent. Their opinion of West Highland seamen is not high. "They've sunk it," he said. "They set off with loads of beer in their bellies when the wind was rising. We asked them to wait until the moon was up. And do you know what they said? One Inishman produced a torch and said he had a moon of his own. The boat was hardly out of Mallaig before it hit the rocks and went down like a bar of soap. We saved the lot of them, including Callum Macrae, which was a grave mistake. Lifeboat practice and no more, you understand." He worked slowly on his net

80

as he talked, an East Coast man who had been in the West Highlands long enough to have lost his sense of time.

"But if you're all that anxious to get to Inish," he said eventually, "there's a boat. Dougal Macphail's is coming in to take some visitors to the protest meeting."

"Dougal Macphail? Protest meeting?"

"They are having some research station for that thing they're always talking about for getting power from the sea. . . . Zeta, is it? And our Nationalist friends will have none of it. There's to be a meeting today and Dougal Macphail is taking the protestors out to the island. Do you know him, then?"

"Yes," I said. During the war, from sheer caprice, Macphail had joined our regiment, instead of the Navy. He had been quickly drawn into the Special Boat Section. Even before the war, his nickname from Oban to Barra was "The Mad Boatman." "If you're determined to go, you'll find Dougal in one of the pubs," the fisherman said.

The pub where I found him was an ambitious shack with a corrugated iron roof, leaning hard against a stone building. It was furnished with ill-assorted kitchen chairs which were gradually and patchily losing their varnish like sunburn; a short, high bar which looked like a disgraced pulpit and which held a glass jar of cold pies; bare wooden floors which were not too closely scrubbed; a smell of boots and whisky. By some eerie combination of the police, the licensing authorities and the low church, many public bars in the Highlands were like this. There was no radio or television, no singing or dancing was allowed, darts were barred in case the more jovial customers should throw them at one another. There were drink and

81

cold pies and that was that.

Macphail was drinking alone, unworried by his surroundings. He had always enjoyed his own company and he had always enjoyed drink. In the battalion it was generally held that he make a drink from metal polish when we were out of milder stuff.

He seemed to suspect me of eccentricity when I said that I couldn't drink on an empty stomach. We small-talked for a bit, and, in his polite and devious Highland way, he did not directly ask me why I had come. Instead he said, "Man, I'm sorry for what I said to you at the theatre that night."

"That's why I'm here," I said, and told him about the trouble. He leaned close, listening theatrically, and I was aware of his warm smile and his cold, watchful eyes.

"So," he said, "you fancy yourself as a rubber-heeler?" The phrase usually applied to a policeman sent to check on another policeman and to get his facts from the underworld. The "rubber-heeler" was disliked by criminals as much as he was disliked by the police. I was an ex-officer, checking up on another officer through sergeants major. I took the point.

"I have to know," I said.

"Knowing will do you no good."

"I have to know. Why do you hate him, for a start?"

"Because he was as two-faced as a cod, a proper chancer. He was a born assassin who lost his nerve and cost us some good men. Will that do you now, Mr. Cameron?"

"What do you mean by a born assassin?"

"The signs were all there," he said, "long before we ever saw action."

According to him, Malcolm was never happier than

82

when he was plowing a hole in something with a burst of machine gun, or using plastic explosives for an ingenious bit of destruction. He even had a ball of plastic explosive he would mold—not play with—mold, into useful shapes. The plastic explosive was safe to handle but it had an unpleasant sickly smell.

"The first time I ever remembered seeing Fleming angry was when a man threw a container of plastic at another man," Macphail said. "It was harmless enough, it wouldn't explode, it was just a silly joke. But the man was joking with explosives and to Fleming, at that time, explosives were sacred. He would go mad if he caught a man with a dirty rifle. You're following me? You don't think I'm too fanciful?"

"I don't know yet," I said. "Did you have any particular assassination in mind?"

"It's too long a story," he said. "I would tell you, right enough, but there's no time now." What he meant was that he would tell it, in his own way, like a Gaelic fairy story with an unpleasant ending or no ending at all. As a professional Highlander, he was in a higher class than Fergus Macdonald. He was well versed in the art which, in an Irishman, might be called bogmanship. "If you'll come over with the party to the island, we'll have an hour or two for talk, then I'll bring you back," he said. This was not my idea; I proposed waiting until night, when he came back to Mallaig.

"There's no place here for serious talk," he said, "and all my maps and documents are on the island." He had a wild, bold, imperious face; he reminded me of Raeburn's portrait of The Macnab.

"You're taking Nationalists," I said.

Macphail looked innocent. An expression of innocence became him as it might have become a vulture.

"What do you mean?" he asked. "I am engaged to take politicians out to the Island of Inish. Nothing will befall them, nothing at all, unless these treacherous bastards on Inish put sugar in my petrol tanks." He seemed determined to have me with him; he wanted an audience. "I'll get you back tonight, certain sure," he said. "There's an especially early meeting for there's no accommodation on Inish for all the riffraff. And anyhow they have to be back at their jobs on Monday morning. Half-time politicians."

I asked him to tell me about Fleming, to make a start.

"What's the hurry?" Macphail asked. "We have the day."

"You knew Malcolm Fleming in Special Boat Section before you were called back to the regiment for the patrol?"

"Not I. But, by all accounts, he was the bloodiest-minded officer we had. From the day we were together, he was forever cleaning his automatic and not letting another man touch it. When he wasn't cleaning his automatic, he was practicing with it. He could aim that pistol better than you or I can aim a fork."

"You're supposed to practice with a revolver," I said.

"True enough, but have you ever known an officer who has seen as much action as he had to go on and on practicing in his own time? Then we were issued with fighting knives and then he started practicing with that. He had the idea that we could learn better how to use the knives at the brigade ration point, cutting the throats of goats for the butchers and so on. Humphries stopped that one; he said it was overenthusiastic."

84

"Poppycock," I said. The bar smells seemed suddenly stronger.

"I can give you the names of the men who'll confirm it."

I would have sworn that I knew Malcolm Fleming very well and that there was nothing in his nature to suggest the bloody-minded, use-cold-steel, frighten-the-Nips-at-night, maim-the-dead-and-deny-the-little-ticks-their-noble-death-in-battle type of officer who flourished in the Burma campaign. The Japanese began this kind of warfare. Perhaps they had forgotten that the British could call upon well-led colonial soldiers who were often better at it. I couldn't see Malcolm Fleming in the part.

"Did you have any particular assassination in mind?" I asked.

He ignored me. "You know that we were going to join the Karens?" he asked. "And that the plane dropped us near a hundred miles from the right place? I'll never forget that march, never."

"I can see that," I said.

"And give the Devil his due, it was there that Fleming showed some of the fine soldiering qualities the man undoubtedly had. He had a special gift for map-reading and for marching on a compass in thick jungle, which is not half as simple as it sounds. It is not a gift you'll claim for yourself, Mr. Cameron? If memory serves me right, you once marched a platoon along the line of a main track for half a day and never found the track?"

"That's right." That day we cut down so much undergrowth that the wits of the platoon were threatening to re-muster in the Forestry Commission. One joker said that if the Japanese were as tired as we were, they wouldn't have the strength to surrender.

"Well, Fleming was different," Macphail said. "By his reckoning we would reach the rendezvous in four days. He was trying to average twenty-five miles or twenty miles a day, and it was a hard walk." This was something of an understatement.

"But Hector Sampson kept me going on the march with a blow-by-blow description of how he bairned his sister-in-law. It was the longest, drawn-out fornication that I ever heard tell of in all my natural days. A buoyant bastard, Sampson. There was not a word of truth in the story, as he admitted to me afterward." But the story took such a grip on him that when he went home he was ashamed to look his sister-in-law in the face. They were short of reasonable water; they'd lost their water-purifying tablets on the drop. "That was the way delirium affected Sampson," he said.

He had me laughing then. By the time I stopped to wonder why Malcolm hadn't made sure that every man had his own water-purifying tablets when they dropped, Macphail was on ahead.

"The theory was," he said, "that we should have been able to dig for safe water in the bed of dried-up chaungs, but Drummond, the doctor with us, wouldn't let us touch that stuff. By the third night we were desperate for water, down to our last two chagals of good stuff, and I was dreaming at night of filling a swimming bath from that burn behind my house and drinking it down."

At dawn on the fourth day when the rest of the patrol was resting, Fleming and he set out with the empty chagals for a stream noted on their map. It was a little close to a village for safety but they had to take the chance. When they got there, they found a pipe of bamboo

86

had been fitted to the stream for easier filling and other signs that told them that the stream was in use.

"On the way back we met a Burmese woman, face to face," Macphail said. "She came out of the undergrowth from a side track that we'd never known was there." Why she was coming for water at that time of the morning he never knew. "But we almost bumped into her and she looked as if she would scream. Before she had the chance, Fleming had her by the throat and then he strangled her. As God is my witness, Mr. Cameron, he strangled her and dragged her into the grass."

"Maybe I'd better have a drink after all," I said.

"Aye, be quick then. And maybe we'll better leave the rest of this until after the meeting. It's not a story I'd want the world to know." There were strangers at the far end of the bar.

8

Most of the visitors for Inish were already waiting by the boat. There were two reporters who, Macphail muttered, were whippet keen and no doubt fresh from uncovering an Egyptian spy ring in Glasgow, anxious to get on with interviewing everything on Inish except the sheep. There was a tall dark woman with a cloak and bonnet of the Mackenzie tartan who, according to Macphail, was a queer Manchester woman who imagined she was Scots. The next arrival was a taller, kilted, bearded Nationalist whom I felt sorry for on sight. He was Macphail's meat. He wore a Balmoral which had a clan badge and a spray.

In his buttonhole there was a small St. Andrew's Cross and—I knew without seeing them—a shoal of Burns Society Badges on the hidden side of his lapel.

"Look at him, will you, look at him?" Macphail asked softly. "I could tell his politics at twenty paces. I wonder where he put his candy claymore?"

It would never occur to him to feel sympathy for such men. They were frustrated dominies, or ministers who distrusted the Church of England, or students who had seen the early Sean O'Casey and fancied themselves in trench coats with automatics in their hands. They'd nothing to do with the men who were working for some possible form of self-government for Scotland. Every one of them saw himself as a future Prime Minister of an independent, sovereign Scotland, making Titoesque deals with Washington and Moscow. As he came on board, the Nationalist removed his Clanranald tie for the sea journey.

"It's tragic, not funny," I said to Macphail. "It isn't fair to jeer at them."

"Tragic figures are often more dangerous than comics," he replied. "Good morning, sir. I'm just waiting for my mate," he roared at the Nationalist. "Will you take your party to the cabin?" He whistled and his mate came on board. The mate was about twelve, Macphail's son. He nodded abruptly at his father and took the wheel.

"Get her started then," the son said coldly to the father, "and don't hang around there yattering."

"Oh ho, he'll be a great seaman," Macphail said.

"Oh, ballocks," his son replied.

The engine was old and tired and slow to start. "She has exotic tastes now," Macphail said. "I have tried her on a hauf and a hauf but she had an Empire builder from Trinidad for an owner once and it's rum and Coca-Cola she's needing."

"Stop practicing your bloody whimsy on me," I said, as I crawled behind him with the oiling can.

The engine started and we left the shore. When we were heading out to sea with the wheelhouse shaking and the thieving seagulls flying escort, I followed Macphail into the cabin. There the passengers were pale.

"Can we go on deck?" the Nationalist shouted. It was the only way to talk, on board.

"No, no, I'm afraid not," Macphail said, solicitous and sorrowful. "I'm a fishing boat, you'll understand, and my insurance is already more than £2 a day but it does not cover passengers or third parties being washed overboard." On deck a giraffe would have been perfectly safe. The elder of the two reporters grinned behind his hand.

"Will it be calm?" the woman passenger asked.

"Oh, yes," Macphail said. "On the way out, I'm sure. I wouldn't be prophetic about the journey back. I thought it would be calm the night the Inish mail boat was lost. Something tragic. Not a man survived. Down with all hands."

"I heard they lived," the Nationalist said.

"Oh, there's a local rumor that they lived," Macphail assured them, "washed up somewhere, living still. It's the beginning of a legend that they lived, right enough, just like Hitler and Lawrence of Arabia." They were not entirely certain that he was joking and the smiles were weak. Then the Nationalist sang, of the island of Islay, in the Gaelic, to keep his spirits up.

"That's the spirit," Macphail said. "Don't let the pros-

89

pect frighten you. Sing flamenco or whatever you like."
By maneuvering his boat, he almost managed to give the
Nationalist a ducking when we landed at the small, rocky
but protected harbor of Inish.

"It's a pity you hadn't a polythene cover for your kilt,"
he said. "It was never much of a maritime rig, the tartan."
It was a bitter joke; Macphail had all the Highland hatred
for Lowlanders who wore clan tartans to which they had
no right.

I managed to get Macphail alone as we walked along
the stones which made a "path" through the bog, between
the harbor and the first of the houses.

"We can duck the meeting," I said.

"No, we can't, but there's a room at the back where we
can talk. I'll make an appearance and slip out, but I have
to be in at the end."

The way to the protest meeting against the Central
Electricity Authority's establishment had been signposted
by the Central Electricity Authority and the meeting was
held on the Authority's land, in the Authority's new hall,
with electricity and water provided by the Authority.
"And you can be sure," Macphail said to me, "that they
will take an efficient note of all the proceedings and behave with perfect fairness throughout." He muttered on;
that was the English all over, he said, a great nation for
creating the appearance of impartiality when they knew
they couldn't lose. Always very tolerant of rebels when the
rebels were impotent. "Whiles they make me want to be
a Nationalist myself. That's my ginger group over there,
led by Callum Macrae."

He pointed, like a detail from the Boyhood of Raleigh,
and several men winked. When the platform party, in-

cluding the Nationalist and the Manchester woman, appeared, he gave them rapt attention, like an ancient, villainous schoolboy.

The hall was still filling, fast. "We can go now," Macphail said, "over there, where it says 'Gentlemen,' that's something of a deception, right enough."

The door marked "Gentlemen" led to a small room with a bench and an open door to the heather.

"Now where were we?" Macphail asked. "The Burmese woman. Well, when we were far enough away and readjusting our loads, I had my first sip of water and then I spoke to him. 'Major Fleming, sir,' I said, 'there's only you and me here and you are a murderous bastard. Put me under open arrest now and when we go back I'll stand court-martial . . . and I'll say it again there. You're a murderous bastard, sir, a born butcher, sir, and for the like of you, war's a rare excuse.'

" 'She would have called for help,' Fleming said. 'There might have been Japanese in her village.'

" 'Aye,' I said, 'and maybe a German armored corps, forbye. You put your hands round her throat to quieten her and then your natural instinct was to kill.'

" 'Did you want me to let her live?' Fleming said. 'How long then would it have been before the Japanese would know that we were here? Even if there wasn't a Japanese patrol in that village at the time.'

" 'Even if you had to kill her, which I doubt,' I said, 'you could have done it a lot quicker and less self-indulgently than yon.'

"The major said nothing to that and we went on. We were just short of our camp when he stopped. 'Do you want to talk about this to the other men?' he asked, and

91

I said 'No.' There was little point in the others knowing the nature of the man they were supposed to trust. 'Then we'll forget about it,' he said, and held out one of his strangling hands."

"He was trying to reason with you," I said, feebly.

"He was feeling guilty, that was all," Macphail replied. "Both my hands were at holding the chagal straps off my weary shoulders, and I kept them there. This sounds like brave talk, Mr. Cameron. Perhaps you think I'm making it up or improving on it a bit?"

"How would I know?" I asked. I didn't think that what Malcolm had done, even if he had done it as Macphail said, would rate as a major war crime. But the action had nothing to do with the Fleming I knew. I remembered a man whom I distrusted on sight. This seemed unreasonable until I saw his expression when he stamped on a stunned bat.

I was brooding about this, while Macphail paused dramatically, then we were aware of a new, powerful voice in the hall. "We'll have to go back now," Macphail said. "Come on."

The speaker was a very young man, dressed in black, and he spoke to the assembled crofters in Gaelic with great effect. "You see?" Macphail said. "A Communist speaking the Gaelic and calling for a gathering of the clans. Now there's an interesting phenomenon if you like." I noted the Doom-is-News delivery and the Billy Graham face.

The speaker saw the English technicians at the back of the hall and changed into English. They would go to prison, on Inish, rather than let the English have their abominable nuclear plant on the island or their murderous bombing planes, he said. The crofters roared approval.

"I thought the crofters wanted to have the research station?" I asked. "It's peaceful? No hydrogen bombs?"

"I thought you knew the islands?" Macphail asked reproachfully. "This is the only entertainment Inish has had for weeks. Television does not cross the Hebridean Sea and the films they see here are old and educational, right enough." There was so much noise in the hall that he could speak loudly. The nation, the Central Electricity Authority were providing the islanders with the finest living that they'd ever known, he said. This was not a reservation for the Lowlanders and these were not Apache that I saw before me. The first protest was genuine enough, meant to raise the price of compensation for the land that the Government had acquired. Now the whole thing was getting out of hand and the Nationalists were complaining so loudly that the crofters were afraid they would not sell the land at all. "They want work," Macphail said. "They are praising this man's gift of words, not his meaning. Shortly now, I'm thinking, the barracking will begin."

There was a certain amount of confusion in the speeches by the locals. According to some, the research station was a Protestant plot to open the door for more Protestants to come in and submerge the old Catholic way of life on Inish. According to others, there was a Catholic plot, for it was well known that many Irish Catholic navvies would come in and so swell the Papist population for the priest to regale in Hebrew or whatever heathen language he used. A third crofter rose and said loudly that both churches were combining to keep humanism and progress from the island.

"Callum Macrae," Dougal said, "the fun is about to begin."

The bearded Nationalist stood up on the platform. "They cannot impose their London will on us," he said. "Nuclear power here and you know what that means. Atomic bombs. A slow death, like that suffered by the Japanese fishermen. English culture proliferating through your glands. . . ."

"The auld sang." Callum Macrae's voice came strongly from the back. "If only I could accompany him. I wish I had my violin."

"And they have a rocket range on Uist," the Nationalist went on. "Why not in London? What would it matter if it went wrong and wiped out London? There would still be forty million of the English. There are only four or five millions of us Scots. We are few but strong in the heart and this island is lovely. . . ."

"Have you tried eating the scenery?" asked another crofter at the back. "And that local slave labor employer up there on the platform beside you. Is he worried about the price the Government is paying for our work?"

"There are servicemen here," the Nationalist went on, "who cannot even speak the Gaelic. . . ."

"We had a bellyful of Gaelic-speaking servicemen at the Massacre of Glencoe," Macrae shouted.

Macphail tapped me on the shoulder. "Macrae is always very immoderate in his language," he said. "He'll be getting thrown out in a minute. Some heavy-handed Nationalists have been camping out on the island for a couple of days. Quick. Get to him."

Macphail had a long reach and he hit out, shouting

94

all the while that he was neutral and being attacked. I had no part in this, but every time I tried to restrain a man, he had moved before I reached him. I felt like a record put on at the wrong speed. We were thrown clear of the hall, when the meeting was breaking up in confusion, when the chairman was shouting, "I take that as unanimous then?" above the din.

We had walked to the Inish lighthouse, which was known to the wittier locals as the Inish night club, before I said, "The police should have been there."

Macphail said that there was one policeman for three islands there and that he was busy when salmon poaching was rife. "He's pestered silly, being the only man tall enough to slip a salmon net across a burn at dead of night."

He led the way. "How long has he been talking like that?" the crofter beside me asked.

"Ever since we left Mallaig."

"And he's to take a boatload of Nationalists back? I fear the worst," he said. "It's the films. The films have done it, the films and Callum Macrae."

It turned out that Dougal Macphail liked films about the Highlands in which either the Highlands were dark and damnable, where floating, trussed-up clansmen in the lochs had their skulls picked clean by gannets; or as high hilarious hills where clansmen broke the boundaries of modern life like affable Apache war parties. When he talked like this, the crofter said, he began to live the part.

9

As soon as we were alone, I said, "Go on, for God's sake, go on. After you got back with the water, after the Burmese woman was dead?"

"When we got back to the patrol, we broke camp right away," he said. "It was easier going after that . . . easier than this in some ways." We were walking over boulders among junk which the islanders had been leaving there for the last twenty-five years. An alder tree, growing among the rock in a wondrous moment of grass, was decorated with two rusting buckets.

"It was only three days then until Fleming got us to the rendezvous," Macphail said. He stopped, with his gum boots firmly planted, for a more powerful delivery. "It was a Karen village where we were treated like heroes and fed on pig and bamboos filled with rice wine. We had to watch that wine. The Karens were sure the Japanese would never get us there, but we still had to watch it. It would never have done to have gone wandering in the jungle, vying with each other with our choruses of the 'Ball of Kirriemuir.' And the headman spoke English. He would have been shocked, the Karens being Christian and worse Bible punchers than ministers in Mull."

On the track above Inish villagers were stopping to watch him, no doubt wondering what commercial notions Macphail had about the garbage heap. We moved on.

96

"How did Ramsay get on with Malcolm Fleming?" I asked.

"Oh, he admired him, admired him—at that time."

"And the doctor who was with you—Dr. Drummond?"

Macphail was able to declaim as we walked; we were on easier ground. "Well, they talked a lot," he said, "specially when we were waiting in this village for a guide to Karen H.Q. And maybe Drummond did Fleming some good." The longer they were in there, the less he saw Malcolm go through the rite of cleaning his revolver. Malcolm found a pool close by, in the strange clicking quiet of young bamboo, and he sat there, sometimes watching a kingfisher at work. He had a diary and he used to write in it closely. He once told me that what he was writing in his diary had nothing to do with the war or the patrol."

"That was reasonable of him, wasn't it? After the way you'd talked to him? And it doesn't sound very much like the zombie soldier you've been building up?"

Macphail spat. "It was always him that talked to me," he said. "I would have as soon cultivated him as I would have asked a hoodie crow in for a bite of supper off my dead dog."

But Malcolm was changing fast, he said. The last thing he expected of him was a show of nerves, but he was "jumpy" on the way to Karen H.Q. with the guiding officer and his men. And yet, when they got there, up on the mountainside, "safe on the heights and the great woolly clouds," Malcolm relaxed again. "Only now and then would we see him walking up and down, with his smile switched off and that strange, dead look on his face," Macphail said. "I see you recognize that mood."

We skirted the main part of Inish village. Although the islanders were solidly behind the research station, Macphail said, hard words had been exchanged between the crofters at the meeting on religion, and before the afternoon was out slander would be flowing faster than the drink. I might know that the man who ran the telephone exchange was Catholic and so the priest knew much of what went out on the lines. Generally, the Protestants did not phone on important business, except maybe to talk about the priest's children, buried in the quicklime.

On the other hand, a Protestant ran the pub and the minister knew about the indiscretions. But, by and large, the Catholics did not use the pub and they would always tell strangers that it was dirty and haunted and sited on some small and perfect shaped stones that were clearly fairy coffins. They also said the manager would lose his license any day, because of his unnatural relations with his pet sheep. "But you're not listening, are you?" Macphail said. "You'll be wanting to hear more about Fleming. Maybe you can't wait until we get to my house."

"Of course I can," I said, unpleasantly. "What's the hurry? We have the day."

His house was immediately beneath a hillock, which had a startling view of Skye, of Loch Coruisk and the hell-folds of the Cuillin, hard and high against the sky. Inish, lying near Soay, has the best view of all of the Cuillin.

The collies walked out, stiff-legged and silent, watching me and then looking at their master for advice. The wife did much the same. She made us a meal of which I ate very little. In the Hebrides, many people seem to live off eggs and buns.

"I will not trouble you too much with what we did with the Karens," Macphail said. "It has little enough part in this story. All I need say is that we did what we were told and made out it was nothing for men of our regiment to drop beyond the Irrawaddy. The Karens, loving the British as they do, thought the world of us. Two things linger in my mind: the pictures of our King and Queen in their bashas, with crossed toy Union Jacks below; and a stray, un-Christian habit that they had for dealing with local traitors and such of the kind. Since the Karens knew they had little enough ammunition to spare, they had the traitors clubbed to death. "Quite ceremonial they were, with the Karen battalions drawn up round the executioner in a square." When the Karens rose, he said, they took ten Japanese for every Karen who died, and he was not surprised at all.

"All right," I said, "very picturesque. What happened next?"

"Well you might ask," he said, "well you might ask. The Japanese got wind of what was going on. They were going to smoke the rebels down from the mountains, before the Karens were ready or armed to act," he said. The Karens were fine soldiers; they could vanish as individual "civilians" and re-form in another place. But the patrol could not. They could consider their assignment at an end, or try to follow the Karens into more difficult country, passing through areas which the Japanese were patrolling heavily. If they considered the task was ended, that they were to play no further part in the Karen rebellion, they would fall back on the British armies, hundreds of miles to the west. It was safer to go back, much safer; even the Karens knew that.

"If we were for back," Macphail said, "a British liaison

99

officer with the Karens would have us picked up by special agents all the way . . . stage by stage. There were enough British cloaks and daggers in Burma by this time for a full-scale fancy-dress ball."

It was Fleming's decision and he had time to make it. Before his patrol moved far at all, he had to take it back to the village where they had first rendezvoused and wait until Japanese activity in the area quieted down.

"And while we were waiting," Macphail said, "the Karens fairly took to Fleming, as people like you did later. They didn't see how nervous the man was. They even inveigled him into coming into the little mission hut they'd kept, despite the Japanese. They got him to give the sermon one Sabbath. They have the legend of a white preacher returning to them. It was an odd sermon Fleming preached, on raising Lazarus from the dead."

Gradually, Japanese activity in the area eased and the British liaison officer with the Karens came down to the village, with his group of Kachin scouts. It was time to move and Malcolm—Macphail said—had still not made up his mind. Malcolm, Ramsay, the liaison officer and Dr. Drummond went into conference in a hut, with a Kachin scout standing sentry at the door.

"You'll maybe excuse me getting close to listen in," Macphail said. "Their voices were raised and, although I'm not normally an eavesdropping man, it crossed my mind that my life was involved in this argument. So I swapped a wink with the Kachin sentry at the door and lay down in the shade beneath the window.

"Naturally the Kachin didn't understand what I was doing. So far as he was concerned, I was seeking shade for a quiet sleep, or what Hector Sampson would call 'Egyptian Physical Training,'" Macphail said. I didn't laugh and Macphail was clearly disappointed, and paused to spit before he went on.

"They were arguing," he said. "Fleming was for going back and saying that the patrol wasn't in good enough heart or health for such a journey. I was surprised at that, right enough. I could see that Fleming had got nervous but I didn't think at that stage that he was yellow." The liaison officer tried to persuade Malcolm to go forward.

"And Ramsay?" I asked.

"He was shocked; he took to hinting that Fleming had lost his nerve. That was the day Ramsay saw through Fleming."

For Macphail, the whole thing was wonderfully simple. Fleming was "yellow." It wouldn't occur to him that any man can do too much, can exhaust his stock of courage. It wouldn't strike him that Malcolm would be able to convince *himself* that the right decision was to go back.

"And Drummond?" I asked. "He would be less emotional than Ramsay?"

"Drummond wasn't really in the argument at all, beyond pointing out, mildly, that the state of our health wasn't all that bad; beyond reminding Ramsay that Fleming was his senior officer. On this matter, the final decision was Fleming's and the doctor knew it."

Macphail was pouring a drink when his wife came into the room. "Are you lonely, my dear?" he asked, softly, grave displeasure in his eyes.

"The people from the mainland are here," she said. "They've heard the radio announcement that the wind is rising and they want to go back now."

Macphail beamed. "An interlude," he said to me, "the thing we were needing. Tell them that my crew is attending to the engines and we cannot start just yet. Tell them the water will be a lot calmer then. Tell them I was maybe wrong in the morning."

"They're threatening to stay on the island if you don't go," his wife said.

"Let them threaten. Remind them that there's no hotel here and that none will put them up, after the behavior of their hooligans. Remind them that the hooligans' tents will go down faster in the wind than any boat of mine." She went.

For Macphail, an "interlude" in the conversation did not mean silence, it meant a change of subject. He said something about Callum Macrae's goats browsing quietly by the Nationalists' tents during the protest meeting, and that Callum Macrae's goats had been known to chew a hawser when they were peckish, but I didn't get it all.

I switched on again, swiftly, when he said, "Then Fleming backed down."

"Fleming did *what*?"

"Fleming backed down. He let the others talk him into going forward to join the Karens, instead of going back to the British lines. The doctor and the liaison officer started off ahead with the bulk of the Kachins and we were to follow, with two Kachin scouts."

"You're *sure* Fleming backed down?"

"I'm sure."

This again was out of character for the man I knew, or the man who had deceived me, or the man I had invented. Malcolm was never indecisive. He might take

102

some time to make up his mind but, when he decided, it was final.

"The morning we set off is very clear in my mind," Macphail said. "We were using a track that the Karens swore the Japanese never used. In all their time in Burma, the Japanese hadn't known that track was there. Not only was it safe but the jungle on both sides was as near as it gets to being impenetrable. To keep off the track was damn near impossible. But Major Fleming hated using tracks, and, having lost his nerve, he made us play at soldiers on it, as if we were Home Guardsmen or something of the kind, practicing the Kitten Crawl before our Sunday joint."

The Kachins, who, he said, knew there would be no Japanese near that track, thought this was some obscure British sport and they joined in. "Have you seen the Kachins?" Macphail asked. "Quite like Gurkhas they are, a soldiering, savage lot if ever there was one, and they had the energy for this game. When we got clear of the track and back into the jungle Ramsay alone was cheery and he took the Bren from me," Macphail said. "The rest of us were a bloody-minded lot. The whole way there had been only one death and only Fleming and myself knew anything about that. For all the rumors, we had heard hunt nor hare of the Japanese and we were beginning to wonder if the Japanese were in Burma at all."

Then they crossed a narrow chaung, or dried-up stream with high walls of shingle and stone and the high trees above that. "It would have been a place to take care in, I'm sure, if we hadn't been exhausted with all the crawling. But for trained soldiers, we were hellish noisy. One Kachin had taken station ahead of us on the side of the chaung and one behind. When the one ahead vanished, we thought he had moved on ahead for a better look at the country.

"Sampson was having trouble with his feet and we were at the back of the column. He was muttering away; he was getting the breeks off his sister-in-law at that particular moment and I was bored with the whole affair."

So Sampson was having trouble with his feet? Perhaps Malcolm had been right about the patrol and the need to go back. For a group of men who were supposed to impress the Karens, their morale did not seem high.

"Then, there was this cracking sound ahead of us, not louder than a squib, and something dropped, a mortar shell it was," Macphail said. "It must have been fired at a steep angle from somewhere close. And it was a 'dud.' They got down on their faces, waiting for the explosion. They waited too long. "The next thing I knew, we were having a taste of machine gun where we lay. We were stuck, finished, due to be murdered to a man and anger was hammering in my head for Sampson. Here I was about to die and, thanks to him, the last thing I would hear of in this world was an elaborate description of the embroidery on this woman's breeks."

It was Ramsay who saved the day, according to Macphail. He was at the front with the Bren gun. He reached the bank, got up and began to fire, shouting to the others to run for cover. "He was a quick-tempered, quicksilver character, reacting the way you would have reacted yourself," Macphail said.

"Thanks," I said, "but I doubt it, I doubt it very much."

"You saw something of the same action in the film, although naturally it was Fleming with the Bren gun

104

on the screen. In fact, he was the fastest man under cover. He showed the rest of us the way, and the flanking fire to cover Mr. Ramsay while he got away, without any orders from Fleming, was provided by Sampson and another man."

I could guess who the other man was. Macphail had always hated to be accused of honorable actions or motives.

"Now, as we discovered late in the war, and as many don't know to this day, the Japanese were lousy jungle fighters, on the whole. The average Japanese private couldn't hit a cow's arse with a rifle on a tripod at thirty yards, and he was easy to confuse in the dark. He was very brave in battle. That was all. There was maybe a company of them there but by dark we were sure that we had all got away." They had lost the Kachin scouts. One had been chopped by the Japanese ambushers. The other had seen the attack. "Maybe he was trying to find us still, maybe he was dead, but if he'd taken a powder and just vanished, thinking we were done for, nobody could have blamed him."

That night the patrol spent in the middle of a thicket of bamboo. "We knew that whatever might get through the bamboo without making a noise like a rhinoceros on roller skates, the Japanese could not," Macphail went on. "For the first time we felt like men on the run and we stayed in the bamboo for the whole of that night." Lieutenant Ramsay and four other men were wounded, all leg wounds. "And Fleming and Ramsay had a helluva row in the middle of the night. They were whispering but fierce, you know? The sentry was certain of it, but he was too far off to hear what they were saying."

On the following day their orders were changed. Not only had Malcolm decided to retreat. He had also decided to split the patrol into two groups, to move always at night.

"When the parties broke up, when Ramsay's syndicate got dressed to go ahead, the source of the argument was clear," Macphail said. It wasn't only that they were retreating and breaking up. Malcolm Fleming had chosen the names for both parties. Ramsay was marching out, wounded, with two of the other wounded and three more men. "I won't bother with their names," Macphail said. "They were the worst men in the patrol and a burden to all of us. There's a lot I could say against these men still, but they are dead."

I could see that Malcolm might have lost the place for a moment, when they were ambushed in the chaung. But this decision was different. Perhaps a man had only to lose his nerve once, as Malcolm had in the chaung—and then he was done.

"The wounded men remaining with us had little wounds. One was Fleming's batman and the other man was the best shot we had, a man with a marvelous gift of getting something for the pot. I'll grant you that my own feelings in this were mixed. I wanted to retreat. I wanted, like God, to be on the side of the big battalions, but there was only one fair way to have split the patrol and that was for Fleming and Mr. Ramsay to have chosen men by turn, the way you do when you're getting a football game going among the lads."

Perhaps Macphail was coloring it. Maybe Ramsay had not seen the choice of men in the same light. Perhaps Malcolm had to be rid of the young officer who at first admired him, then had contempt for him, then refused to take orders.

"Did you speak to Ramsay about this?" I asked Macphail.

"I did. 'You're not going to put up with this, sir?' I asked, and he said, 'That I am' or something of the kind, words that better suited his accent and his mouth. 'I am,' he said, 'and when I get out, not if I get out, when I get out, Major Fleming's for court-martial. He's not only keeping all the best unwounded men and the best weapons; he's hanging on to the only compass left.' I asked him to stay. It was a fine point of military procedure but I didn't see how Major Fleming could drive him off on his own.

"'Well, it's an order,' Ramsay said, 'and although I've got the lame and the lazy, I'm very pleased to go.' He was young, you know, and maybe his Gary Cooper stand with the Bren gun had gone to his head, but to go without a compass with this mob of the walking wounded, the cowardly and the work-shy was crazy, right enough."

Ramsay set off before it was dark. The others were to follow the next night.

"He got maybe half an hour on his way. And then we heard noises. Faint though they were, we recognized them." It could have been that the Japanese platoon which had ambushed them on the night before were waiting on the line of retreat. "Or maybe a certain nameless man drew them with a habit that he had of shouting out in fear at every shadow," Macphail said. "When he was chosen for this caper he had seemed a good man more than likely. And, including Fleming, there were only four worthless bastards on our whole patrol. The

107

rest were soldiers. In the history of war, that is a fair enough average, is it not?" The extra little twist on this, he said, was that if Ramsay had been with the others, marching dead on a compass bearing, he would have been nowhere near that ambush spot.

"There were one or two things to do," Macphail said. "We could try to create a diversion and give Mr. Ramsay's men a chance to melt. Or we could stay where we were. One of us, Sampson I think it was, volunteered to have a go at doing something for them.

"'Stay where you are,' Fleming said. 'All you'll do, blundering through that bamboo, is to bring them down on us. This patrol must stay together. None of us will survive if we try to act in little groups.'" What Fleming had said made sense, but it also made nonsense of his order to split the patrol in two. "I had feared the old Fleming as a butcher who had no respect for his own life or that of any other men," Macphail said. "But the old Fleming would never have split the patrol that way, had he split it at all. Nor, when his men were ambushed, would he have lain there. He would have been up, in close, killing or being killed, with a good military excuse to back that decision, too."

"A helluva decision to make," I said.

"It was that," Macphail went on, "but there were other decisions to come. When the firing was all over and some time had passed, Sampson and another man happened to go down there in the dark. We . . . they . . . were not disobeying orders, you'll understand." They just happened to think that they were heading toward water, having been told to fill the chagals, and they had missed the way and gone in that direction, still searching for water, quite by chance. Then they were drawn by the voices, that was all, Macphail said.

"I'm not giving details of this to you or any other man. Mr. Ramsay and one other man were still alive and there were no more than one Japanese N.C.O. and ten men amusing themselves with them. The rest of the ambush party had gone. Sampson and the other man were certain of that. There was no doubt at all. They must have been a pretty hairy mob of Japanese not to have kept Ramsay for interrogating; a low-browed lot, altogether." The Japanese were so sure that this was the last of the British patrol that they had only one keen sentry posted. Their rifles, "proper Crimean War pieces too," were stacked as if it were a barrack room. "There was never a finer rifle, or a Bren gun, target, firing single shots, you'll understand, specializing in the belly or the privates," Macphail said. "But these two men had only Sten guns, with an effective range of—what—thirty yards? They would have joined Mr. Ramsay." The keen sentry had an automatic rifle.

They got away. Macphail didn't reckon it was difficult with the noise that was going on and they told all this to Malcolm. "Now my story could be the story of an embittered man but, if you don't believe me, Mr. Cameron, every bloody man who survived was there at the next bit. I can give you most of the names and even the addresses if you want them." Macphail was cutting tobacco while he talked. He made a mess of it; his hand was unsteady. He said that Malcolm told the men that they were fools to imagine there were only eleven Japanese there. From what they'd said, Ramsay and the man were not to have much time left and he would not throw the rest of the patrol after them.

"When one of the two men tried to swap his Sten gun

for a rifle, and when Sampson offered to carry the Bren gun, out of his turn, they did it quietly, you'll understand," Macphail went on. "What they had seen would take the bravado and the boasting out of any man. They were just off for another search for water, having failed to find it in the first place." Macphail began to dig at the table with his knife.

"Fleming put them under open arrest and he backed his order with his favorite, clean .45 Colt of his in his hand," he said. "This was how far a major of our regiment had to descend to have an order carried out. The men pointed out to him that he was bluffing, that he would never fire and alert the Japanese. And he answered, a small arms expert to the last, that his automatic was quiet and the wind was in the wrong direction. Any questions, Mr. Cameron?"

"No," I said, "no questions."

So that was the end of that, according to Macphail. He remembered three things only on the march out, three things worth passing on. One he'd told me already: Ramsay would have been nowhere near where he was ambushed if he'd been marching on a compass, "handled with the special skill of Major Fleming."

The next was of being stung by a scorpion when they were wading in the mud of a paddy field in monsoon. "And I thought, 'Well then, that's a scorpion bite and it's painful but I'll survive.'" The third was when they were hungry, when Macphail had used his last round of Sten-gun ammunition. He stood within a room length of a great deer that would have made a feast for all of them.

"Did I say three? There were four. The fourth thing was to report Major Fleming when we got back. For

110

weeks and weeks Sampson and me fattened on the thought of his court-martial. The thought kept us going as it must have kept Mr. Ramsay going on his last day alive. Maybe that was why we worked so hard to get Fleming out of Burma."

In hospital they realized that they could have left him, but it was not for them to bring him back for punishment. At the court-martial, too, it would come out how Ramsay and the others died and their next-of-kin would have known. Macphail admitted that their evidence would not have made a certain case against Malcolm.

"He could say in all honesty that Sampson had once fallen asleep on sentry go and that I had been mutinous after he strangled the Burmese woman," Macphail said. "And that strangling was another thing he could have justified. It was then that Sampson and myself and the others made this bond, not to say anything about the patrol beyond answering the few official questions we might be asked."

The Special Service war was over for them and they went back to the battalion. "Some of it leaked out, right enough, and I've always thought that Humphries, far less of a fool than he looks and talks, had built up quite an ugly picture of it all; using the regimental sergeant major to put innocent-sounding questions to the others who survived. On Sergeants' Mess Nights, no doubt, when the drink had eaten at the hinges of their tongues," Macphail said. None of the patrol members was ever in Malcolm's company, or even in his presence if it could be avoided.

"And then there was the film?" I said.

"Yes, then there was the film.

111

"The years rolled by. I heard hunt nor hare of Fleming again until I saw this film, this weird and wonderful version of the patrol, with himself the modest, bashful hero of it, with Mr. Ramsay the man he tried to save, and myself the simple loyal Highlander who served Fleming, from my deep sheep-love for him. We were even in the Karen rising, according to the film."

Macphail maintained that he wasn't consulted "properly" about the film. He'd had a letter from the film company saying that a film was to be made and did he mind signing the accompanying chit to the effect that it was all right to use his name if they kept to the facts and didn't malign him? "Mug that I was, I signed it and Sampson did the same. Some of the others signed for money, others from vanity like Sampson and me. Nobody mentioned that Fleming was the 'technical advisor.' We thought we would be asked to help, and that it might be interesting at that, sticking to the first half of the journey."

When Macphail saw the film he considered consulting a lawyer. "But it would have been the same old story all over again. Lieutenant Ramsay's mother and the others would have found out how they had died. We'd have been standing in the witness box attacking a dead man and the newspapers full of the whole affair. I'm afraid the others raised a hullabaloo."

"You don't think that Fleming could have been fooled like the rest of you?" I asked. "He has to be the villain for every act? He couldn't have given an honest version of . . . anyway . . . the first part of that patrol and left it at that? He couldn't have been trying to give credit where credit was due? Then been tricked like the rest of you, tricked when he was dead?"

"It's possible," Macphail said.

I asked for Dr. Drummond's address and he gave it to me. The doctor had given up medicine and he was farming in Argyll. Dougal said that he would write and tell the doctor I was coming. "Without putting thoughts against Fleming into his mind?" I asked. "You don't know the doctor," he replied.

It was more than time to go. I could tell by the noises at the door that the Nationalist and his company were there. Had I been the Nationalist, I wouldn't have sailed back with Dougal Macphail for all the Sabbaths on Inish, nor all the pressing appointments with work and Monday morning, not if I had to sleep in the heather with Callum Macrae's goats nosing round me. But the Nationalist was a romantic in his fashion, with a strange faith in Highland nature.

I couldn't worry about the journey back. Macphail's story had a deadening effect on me. For all his phrasing I thought that he had been telling the truth as he knew it.

"He wasn't even paid for his advice on the film," I said. "Oh, he wouldn't be paid, I wouldn't suppose. He was always Big Mick, the man for the grand gesture. He was maybe shorter of fame, hungrier for the glory than he was for money. In the years between, he maybe talked himself into believing that what he said was what happened."

"Dougal!" his wife shouted. "Come on, come on. It's past the time. And your son's down in the Bilge making a fool of himself." The only public house on Inish was known far and wide to seamen as the Bilge.

"It's always *my* son when there's trouble," he said.

113

10

We sailed from Inish into a curtain of rain when the wind was rising. Skye, so near and clear an hour before, was a shapeless bank of mist.

"None of your tricks," I said to Macphail. "I have to get to Mallaig tonight. I have to. I've got a nervous woman waiting."

But he was already back in his role of the Ancient Gaelic Mariner and he answered, with a wealth of sadness in his beer-stained eyes, "It is the misfortune of the likes of you and me always to have nervous women waiting. We will make the shore," he said. "We'll make the shore although my crew has deserted me." He pointed contemptuously at his son, who lay in drunken sleep on the wheelhouse floor. "A waste, the drink, on him," he said, "a shocking waste. When he is old enough to be allowed in the pubs of Mallaig, he will disgrace us all."

For the next fifteen minutes, I stayed below to keep dry. It was so calm in the lee of the island that the passengers took heart and the female Nationalist told me all about her Nationalist father, who was eighty-two and, as he said, "prematurely white but committed to a policy of nonviolence in the struggle for freedom." He wanted Home Rule for Scotland but he denied the right of the "English" Parliament to grant it to us. The bearded Nationalist did not laugh.

He told us about a talk he had given to some islanders. "And what," he'd asked them, "would the history of the world have been if Scotland had not had a patriot like Bruce to rise up?" He gave the names of two of the islanders. The Bruce was a traditional black enemy of their clan, with something of the reputation Cromwell had in Ireland. The Bruce was a Sassenach, forbye. I wondered if Dougal Macphail found me and my friendship for Fleming as ridiculous as he found the Nationalists.

Only the younger of the two reporters had come back with us from Inish. He was a keen lad of about nineteen, with his pencils sharpened at both ends and a soft hat on the back of his head. He would have had a ticket saying PRESS in his hat-band, had he dared. The reporter seemed bored with the talk of Nationalism, in search of something more exciting.

"Mr. Macphail said you're in television," he said.

Even in a boat off Inish, there was no escaping television; it had traveled world-wide. There were sets in the market squares of old Bagdad, the Puerto Rican signal reached the Virgin Islands, softs winds stirred the aerials of Hawaii. There were neither flies nor television sets in China, but there were an awful lot of viewers in Brazil.

"B.B.C. or Independent?" the reporter asked.

"Independent," I said, and he was off. Did I think that Independent had more influence, more viewers than the B.B.C.? I didn't know. At the time, both sides in television were still trying to establish their superior strength by brandishing the most suspect statistics since the digit-happy days of economic warfare. By comparison the road accident figures, the juvenile delinquency charts, the divorce rates and the cost of living indices were miraculously exact.

"The Scottish Independent service isn't very Scottish,"

the reporter said. "From the start, network stuff. What's so Scottish about Meet the Stars in Blackpool or Emergency Ward 10? What's so . . ."

He stopped as the boat shuddered.

By my reckoning, we could not yet have hit rough water but, with seamanship and his knowledge of the currents, Dougal made his boat behave like a drunken funfair steamboat. We tried to ignore it and, after a while, the reporter began again. He had an idea for a serial on Rob Roy MacGregor in twelve installments. There would be a comic foot gillie, a clan gathering jingle and a script stuffed with words like "mislike," "speckled trout," "oxter" and "jalouse." . . .

He stopped again when the cabin danced.

"Or do you think I'd have to modernize it more," he said, when things were quieter, "for overseas audiences? God Almighty, what's that?"

My first impression was that we had turned over. When I felt a little better, I went on deck, followed by the reporter and the female Nationalist. The reporter had forgotten Rob Roy, and he wanted to know if there was an air-sea rescue station in the area. Air-sea rescue always made a headline, he said.

I joined Douglas in the wheelhouse while he took station with the woman in the bows. As Rum rose suddenly from the mist, like a surfacing sea serpent, the woman pointed to it. "First Uist, then Inish," she said. "They'd even spoil this island, this lovely island of Canna." The speech was remarkably clear, and it was obvious that she had a strong stomach when she began to sing "Scots, Wha Hae" loudly, competing with the waves, the wind and the agonized old engine which seemed to be trying to batter its way out of the boat, to die in freedom.

116

"Enough of that, madam," Macphail shouted. "We want no massed choir effects at this time of peril. This is not the *Titanic*." Again I asked him to behave and he nodded. "Go down below and see how her friend is getting on," he said. "I have a feeling that he will not come back to Inish, not even when the sea is smoother than his tongue."

The Nationalist was alone in the cabin. "I knew it would be bad," he said, "but I have to go back tonight. Promise me we'll make the shore. Promise me we'll land."

"Oh, we'll land," I said. "Come on. You'll be better on deck. Come on, I'll give you a hand. It's just possible that Macphail is exaggerating the dangers of this voyage." He was not easily persuaded and, by the time we reached the deck, we were in the storm and the boat seemed to have changed direction. I asked Macphail, who pretended not to understand, but we were certainly running into wilder water. The mouth of a loch? It couldn't be. Even Macphail in his craziest mood would not go hours out of his way, and perhaps even endanger his boat, to terrify his passengers among the rocks of Skye. . . .

The mist suddenly parted and for a moment I saw a view I knew too well, as terrible as any that I've seen, the Cuillin in the rain. We were heading for the rocks of the loch where nothing lived. "What's the bloody game?" I asked. "You're beginning to frighten the hell out of me now and in a minute you'll be seeing how far you can go without passing out, yourself. You brave boys are all the same, pushing it too far because you're so terrified of being afraid. This is not the craft for this caper and you know it. What's the bloody game?" I understood one thing more, one of the most hellish strains on Malcolm on that last patrol must have been trying to cope with the daft bravado of people like Sampson and Macphail.

117

"The wind is driving us this way," he said.

"You're a treacherous, lying bastard. The wind is doing nothing of the kind."

"Treacherous I may be, Tom Cameron, and a liar to boot. But bastard I am not. If you cannot moderate your language, I will ask you to leave the bridge." The boat was rolling now; at this stage of its life it was not fit for such work. Sometimes the wheelhouse seemed to touch the water as it rolled. When it was calm for a moment, I got the other passengers below, then climbed to the top of the gangway and hung on with only my head above deck. I had to push the reporter down; he was complaining all the time about interference with the freedom of the Press.

"Tell them where the lifebelt is," Macphail said, smiling like a dogfish. "Always better to be on the safe side."

"Go and stuff yourself," I said. "Go and boil your can. Of all the idiotic . . ." The engine had stopped and I could only assume that Macphail had finally gone mad. There was no point in swearing at him. Gentleness and flattery were required.

It was easier now to reach the wheelhouse. "Dougal," I said, "I've never known the like of this. Steering in this sea, in this mist, among these rocks, without an engine. It will be the talk of Mallaig. Let's get back there, before the pubs are closed."

He swore, deeply and terribly, in the Gaelic. "Do you think I'm a magician?" he asked. "Stopping the engine from the wheelhouse?"

His son had been sliding limply and easily on the floor of the wheelhouse, like a dead fish. I got him sitting up and then I began to shake him. The boy opened his eyes and smiled vaguely. "The engine's stopped," his father said.

"That so? Fancy that," the boy said, and closed his eyes again. He pressed his back against the wheelhouse wall, stretched his arms and pressed his hands hard against the wood. Then he rocked, with his eyes closed.

"Are you still enjoying the joke?" I asked Macphail. "Are you hoping to die laughing? Always leave them laughing." I was beginning to stammer with anger.

He shrugged. "I know this loch better than I know the back of my hand," he said. "I bring the English tourists here, whiles. Marvelous it is watching them, better than going to the zoo. We're drifting in, just nicely, as we are. I can beach her, easy, if you'll help me."

"We will," the reporter said. "Is this a record? Is this the first time this has happened?"

The Nationalist in the cabin was too ill and remote to have understood what was happening. I told him and tried to reassure him then and he was good enough to nod. At that moment he would have been happy to land in the Antarctic.

Macphail beached the craft, almost as easily as he'd said, on the shingle, inside a horseshoe formation of rock. In time, the wind lost its force and the rain slackened. On the iron-range fire in the center of the cabin we made tea and revived young Macphail. Then he worked solidly on the engine without success. He was still working when the late sun came up.

"I'm needing something to eat," the boy said sullenly.

"And you could have had it too, had you not wolfed the emergency sandwiches," his father said. "You have no moral fiber when it comes to cream cheese." We worked on for an hour. "There is one man in these parts that can fix this," Dougal said at last, "and that's a man at Glen

Brittle. He has the touch with engines, right enough. He could start this heap of festering junk with a corkscrew and a bottle of hair tonic, if the mood was on him. That's if you can fetch him, Mr. Cameron. You're the great harrier of this lot."

"Walk to Glen Brittle?" I asked. "To the other side of the Cuillin? There might be help coming out, for all we know. The weather's cheering up. They might have seen us from Elgol."

"I don't think so," Macphail said, "and I hope not. I am no friends of the Elgol boatmen. You'll know their version of the 'Skye Boat Song' which is 'Baksheesh, baksheesh, ah ah.'" For all he knew, they would claim to be salvaging. "I would ask for a tow from a basking shark before I went to them. Win over the hill to Glen Brittle, unless you want to spend the night here. Remember that nervous woman of yours, waiting."

The sun was strengthening, the light lasted long at this time of year, the evening would be fine. "Round the edge of the hills?" I asked.

"Are you daft? If you don't know your way round you'll end up on the headland and wading up to your knees half the time. Have you water and provisions for a fortnight? If you know the Cuillin at all—and I think you know it—go up and over the top. Up there there's a clear path all the way. It looks frightening, I'll grant you, but a sure-footed man will have no trouble."

When the young reporter volunteered, I knew I had to go. I set off alone, toward the gap which was one of the so-called tourist routes across the Cuillin. I walked toward it steadily for a quarter of an hour, hesitated, set off again, then stopped when I was well out of sight of the boat.

120

I couldn't face it. I had been over the ridge on such routes before, with others, and I'd had no great difficulty in climbing or coming down. But, sitting in perfect safety on top, I had been very much afraid, not of falling, I thought, simply afraid. I'd had to force myself to look while a friend had danced on the ridge, pointing out at Barra and Rum and Canna, slanting down into the great chasms below him. I had a spiritual, rather than a physical fear of the Cuillin Ridge. I had been on it three times, trying to kill the fear, finding it growing stronger. Now I couldn't face it alone, nor could I admit my fear to Macphail.

As I turned away, searching for a track which would run round the ridge between the mountains and the headland, I tried to convince myself that this was a better way, because the rock might be wet, because I was wearing crepe-soled shoes, because there was an outside chance of the rain and mist returning, but I knew that the very steep grass slopes above the plunge of cliff into the water would be as treacherous in the wet, my shoes as dangerous there, the chance of getting lost greater if the bad weather came back.

I was turning away, simply—and simple was the word —afraid of the Cuillin Ridge as the old Highlanders I found so funny were afraid of the Little People; this, after judging Malcolm Fleming who had been a brave man once.

At first I walked on a steep grass slope, slipping occasionally, but reassured by the sight of grass and more grass far below. Then the track faded out and I could not get a proper grip with my shoes. If I tumbled, I might not be able to stop quickly, but a long slide through the

121

grass could not hurt. I stopped, walked on for a little, slid for some way and stopped again.

My legs were trembling and I was tired and I had eaten very little that day.

It seemed better to go down, to lose height and direction for the sake of flatter, easier walking on the slopes below. On the way down the slope I was forced to walk fast, then slide, stumble, slide on for most of the way.

I was sliding, happier, whistling, when a large round stone broke loose. I watched it, expecting to see it bounce to the bottom. The stone gathered speed and then it vanished and crashed a long way below. I guessed that it had found a narrow crack, but I took it more easily to make sure, trying to find secure footholds, working away from the path the stone had traveled. This was too slow and I began to slide again. Then I stopped, grabbing at the grass, swept by panic.

I was almost on a convex rock face, so steep and smooth that I had not seen it from above, so steep that I'd had the illusion that the grass I was sliding on led straight to the grass slope hundreds of feet below. The rock was very smooth and round. Was this what real climbers called boiler plate?

There was very little danger of falling over and I knew it. I could crawl back up the steep grass, on hands and knees if I chose, use my teeth if I liked, with no one to see me at it. But the boiler plate was frightening, just by being there.

So I lay there for some time, digging my heels in, holding hands with the grass; and, when I got up, I walked straight up the slope, away from the rock face, hoping to go round the shoulder of the hills until I saw a path down into Glen Brittle.

I was breathing heavily. Besides being tired and hungry, I had drunk too much, eaten too little, smoked too much in the years since I walked the long paths through safer hills.

Before I got to the top, I heard the sea. Then I made it, looked down, and began to swear. To save a walk across the Cuillin Ridge, I had traveled miles out of my way on an ankle-torturing slope with boiler plate on one side and this on the other—a deep gully in the keeping of the sea. Far below water foamed in broken black rock which looked as if it had been lifted then dropped like a tray of crockery. From this height it was not easy to judge how wide it was, how fast or how deep. The rock was very steep on both sides. It would be a long, long walk round it—and I'd run away enough. Pretty soon I'd be scampering like a frightened rat, in circles.

I had not been walking on the main headland or the shoulder of the Cuillin, but on a neck which led at best to Loch Scavaig or the Soay Sound. I could either go back, almost as far as the boat and face Macphail—or cross this. The far side looked the steeper but there were cracks which might go the whole way.

I had never learned to work out a route on rock or to go down properly with my face toward it. I began to slide and struggle, resting when I reached an overhang, throwing rocks and cursing Skye before I found a new way down. I sweated until my clothes were soaked and shivered when the wind got at the sweat. The funny thing was that I did not get frightened.

Above, the boiler plate had not been dangerous. Here

I had only to go down too far in the wrong direction and that was my lot. Somehow it seemed easier, so much easier that I soon reached the bottom.

I rested there, flat out in a wet patch of heather which brushed rain into my skin and clothes every time I moved, looking up into the sky. Then the first golden eagle I'd ever seen in Scotland crossed the mountain in one effortless glide. All my life I'd been frightened of the wrong things at the wrong time. Maybe that had once happened to Malcolm.

Whatever the film company or the survivors or the newspapers might want to do about his last patrol, I had to go on and find out *why* he had done what he had done. There was no need for me to award Malcolm so many marks out of a hundred as a soldier, or as a human being. The only thing was to find out what had happened, to try to understand what he was trying to do. What do they hunt, the velvet tigers in the jungle?

The water wasn't difficult to cross. Jumping from rock to rock, I missed my footing only once and went in, but it was shallower at this part, about waist deep. Half wading, half pushed by the fast water, I reached another stone, then the shore and the heather which led to what looked like a crack which would lead to the top, with any luck. It was easy going in the heather and the crack began well enough. Then it became steadily more steep and smooth, with fewer and fewer handholds or places where I could put my wet soles without sliding. I had seen pictures of climbers in a "chimney" putting their feet against one wall of rock, pressing their backs against the other and slowly working their way upward—or something like that. I tried this for the first time and found it slow, perhaps because I

124

was not deliberate enough, perhaps because my knees would not stop trembling. Then I found a part of the crack where I could wedge myself and look for another route. There didn't seem to be one; the rock seemed more and more like a tiled wall; I felt as if I was being watched, like a flitted fly trying to climb a fireplace. When I looked sideways for long I got dizzy, so I looked down between my feet and quickly back at the rock on eye level and I tried to think, control the panic. Why be sorry for cowards and contemptuous of brave men who faltered?

"The Leith police dismitheth us and it suffitheth us," I said to the rock, and began to work my way up the crack again. My movements were panicky at first, but the rough rhythm gradually revived me.

Then I slipped.

For a moment or two I was falling through air, then I began to bounce on rock and tried to claw at it.

I was saying. "The Leith Police . . . the Leith Police . . . the Leith Police . . ." when my head hit something hard and it was dark.

11

I spluttered then coughed it up. "Stop burning my throat," I said.

"Burning your throat be damned," someone said. "That's brandy. Christ, he's fit enough already to complain about the quality of the drink. Some fellahs have a' the luck. Bet he hasn't even twisted his ankle. Listen, Mac. You ought to be deid."

125

"Shut up. Shut up and leave him alone," a second man said. "He's maybe sufferin' from shock."

"Nothing like the shock Ah got when he spat up the brandy." I opened my eyes warily. There were two climbers.

"Where were you, Mac?" one asked. "Were you on that rock on your own without a rope or decent gear, or were you trying your hand at low flying?"

"Will you belt up?" the other said. "Will you put a sock in it? Are you all right, Jock?"

"All right," I said. "Think so." I was still in sodden clothing, with blankets wrapped round me and something hard, a rucksack frame, at my head.

"Don't try to move. Give me that brandy. Open your mouth, Jock. This'll do you good. That's right. Get the tea, Harry."

"One minute Ah'm a mountain goat. The next Ah'm a St. Bernard. Now Ah'm a waitress. Milk and sugar, Mac? The scones are lovely, the day."

"Shut your gob. Never mind him, Jock. Yatter, yatter, yatter when he's worked up. You had us worried. Sure you're all right? Hold his head up while I pour this tea into him."

"There's a boat in Loch . . . in the—" I began.

"We know that, we know that. Just drink this tea; the stretcher will be here in a minute."

"Stretcher?" I sat up quickly and the tea poured down the blanket. I was stiff, very stiff, but so far as I could make out nothing was broken. My head was very sore and I lay back again.

"That's it, Mac, take it easy. Your flying-trapeze act is over. Lie back. Ah've got one dry fag. Open your mouth careful like. Ah'm not wasting this on the heather."

I lay still and smoked while they talked about how lucky I had been. If a climbing party sheltering high in the storm had not seen Macphail's boat when the mist cleared, if they had not seen me setting off in the wrong direction, when they were heading for the boat . . .

"You're haunted, Mac, you're haunted. If we hadn't seen you, you were done for. Were you going to *swim* back to the mainland? What was the idea of trying that cliff? Did you fancy your chance as a Sherpa?"

I raised my head and began to get up. "Sorry," I said, "very sorry. I don't know how to thank you. I think I can walk."

"A long walk, Mac. We're waiting for a boat with the stretcher. Sit down."

When the stretcher party came up the gully they seemed disappointed that I did not need them. I was led, still wrapped in blankets, like a captive Indian, to the mouth of the inlet and there the boat was waiting, with Macphail to welcome me on board.

"What was the game?" he asked. "You brave boys are all the same, pushing it too far. I get the engines fixed, then I have to come and look for you. What was the game? Were you planning on a picnic with the Weird Sisters of Coruisk?"

"Macphail, I'm just not strong enough to kick you where it hurts." He grinned.

"Soon as we get you into dry clothes and this lot off to Glen Brittle, we'll have you looked at at the hospital in Mallaig."

"He's maybe not up to it," one of the climbers said.

"I'm up to it."

127

"Oh, he's up to it. I get a special rate for transporting the island sick and wounded to the hospital in Mallaig. I will never hear a word said against the National Health Service."

There was no sign of the reporter; the Nationalists had elected to stay on Skye, Sabbath or no Sabbath, and ignore the Monday morning call to work. We had a quiet, calm journey back to Mallaig with Macphail at the wheel while the boy nursed the engine. It struck me that my most cowardly act of the day was not to have admitted my fear of the Ridge.

"I'll better tell you, Dougal. I didn't go over the Gap because of sheer black superstitious fear. The Cuillin gives me the creeps. I wouldn't expect a brave, bold character like you to understand that."

"No? Well, I do. I have that fear myself. Had you told me at the time I would have understood. Are you a Highlander then, after all?"

My name is Highland but our family history is not, as far as I can trace it back, to my grandfather and no further. My home town lies on the Highland Line but the Highland Line of the geography books tramples down the heather and the history, wandering freely from the facts. Whether people in our town declare themselves to be Highland or Lowland is entirely a matter of the emotion of the moment. The town was never Highland to a Highlander. It was a town where they cheerfully hanged wounded stragglers from Highland cattle-raiding parties, a town the Highlanders happily put to the fire and the sword on every major uprising. But pride in the Highlander and his old fierce ways has been spreading south ever since he was humiliated and finally disarmed, ever

128

since we betrayed him to the English.

"I don't know, but I've got a Highland imagination when I'm scared for my skin. It helps to make me understand what Malcolm Fleming must have gone through. He maybe had one of those private fears, like the fear of the Cuillin, something you others didn't know about, something that was hard to control."

"What I'm thinking is this. If I could prove to you that Malcolm Fleming had gone in for skinning babies, you would come up with an argument in his favor. Loyalty's a terrible thing."

"Did you never try to find out what was wrong with him, even at the start?"

"Oh, aye," Macphail said, "I was interested in the man. One night at the end of training I got him going on a bottle of firewater. He seemed to have very little interest in life. When he got drunk he even said that he hoped to have one last leave in Kashmir before he got the chopper."

"'The chopper?'" I asked him. "'Sir, there's years and years of life in you yet.'"

"I was far too quick with it; that was the end of the conversation. In the morning he dropped a hint about overfamiliarity in that easy, friendly, take-no-offense manner that he had."

"This 'no interest in life' stuff is a bit strong," I said. "He was married before he went East. What did he say about his wife?"

Macphail looked at me, genuinely surprised. "Are you sure? Are you sure? He never mentioned a wife. I always thought he was married afterward."

They kept me in the hospital that night and let me out after breakfast. The only way a patient ever escapes from

129

hospital before breakfast is by death. Then I hired a car and drove inland to Ruth's "bothy," which was a large, stone cottage with wide, converted windows, overlooking the sound and the unlikely tusked island of Eigg, like a rhino browsing in the water.

I was paying off the driver, on the turning place beneath the cottage, when she came running out, head forward, heels too close as she lifted them; the usual fast, sexy stumble. She put her arms round my neck. "Oh, you're safe," she said, "you're safe." She made me feel like an Appin Stuart who had marched to the walls of Inverary and had been saved from the Campbell swords.

She took in the head bandage, which was covering a mild graze. "I knew it, I knew it," she said. "Even before the paper came I knew that something was wrong. I didn't know what and I didn't know where, but I knew that something was wrong."

"What newspaper?" I asked, crossing the threshold with her. She had never claimed the Second Sight before. There was a Scottish Sunday newspaper on the table, ferociously parochial in content, to compete with the great Sundays of the South.

The headline was:

SKYE DRAMA:

SCOTS TV PRODUCER RESCUED
Glasgow Men Find Him Delirious

It turned out that I was a "well-known Scottish-born TV producer, that I had been taken to Mallaig by helicopter and that Dougal Macphail, a "kenspeckle figure in Mallaig," had taken part in the air-sea rescue. Late last night Mallaig hospital had reported that I was out of danger.

130

"When I phoned the hospital, you'd left," Ruth said. "Tell me about it; tell me all about it." She understood my fear; she listened to that bit, leaning forward, with her hands outstretched and touching at the fingertips; she'd had that fear herself, one night on the An Teallach hills when the moon was playing tricks with twisted rock. But she hadn't much to say about the fears that might have been on Malcolm, when I told her what Macphail had said. She listened closely enough, but she seemed to be more interested in how I was reacting than in reacting herself. That was that, she said; the film company would probably hush it up. I ended up looking away from her, out from her window toward the seaweed beach at Arisaig. Along the road were the long, lovely sands of Morar. Closer there was a railway poster advertising the beach at Blackpool.

"I had this funny feeling when Macphail was talking," I said. "It didn't last long, but while he was talking he made me feel that I'd never known Malcolm, at all."

"Well, did you?"

"I didn't know the man Macphail knew. Sometimes it seems I didn't know the man you knew."

She came and stood behind me. She could always distract any line of thought, even this one, by standing close behind me. "You saw him once every two months, every three months, for how long? An evening? When he had some anecdotes, some more ideas, he picked up and literally pecked to death. He could be the whistling, smiling boy with you: the bright, eager brain."

"You don't want to talk against him, do you? Not that kind of woman. Just every time you mention him, you manage to put down poison."

She said, "I think I'd better go and make the lunch."

131

I didn't turn round until she'd left the room, then I settled down with the Scottish Sunday paper.

The report of next importance to my dramatic rescue concerned a very grave situation in Berlin. The American and Russian statements had been so threatening that it looked as if there might have to be another Berlin airlift. In Berlin there was half a battalion of Scottish troops and the headline on this account of a crisis which might shake the world was GORDONS IN DANGER.

On the next page there was a half-column report of the protest meeting on Inish and, according to this report, the decision of the meeting had been unanimous. It was headlined INISH DEMANDS THAT ENGLISH GO. The scuffle, the heckling, were not mentioned. Even in anti-Nationalist editors, the fear of treachery can be as strong as it is in the Soviet Writers' Union.

It all reminded me of Macphail's version of the last patrol. Ruth must see that it did not add up. I went to look for her.

Just as I reached the kitchen she dropped a box of matches and she did not simply bend to pick them up, she dropped almost on one knee and reached for the matches, still holding her head erect. She saw me staring and held the position for a second, looking like a figure in a parents' night Girl Guide tableau.

"Sorry," Ruth said, as she got up. "This probably looks silly. But it's something I saw demonstrated on television. A man said that women give themselves awful backaches with the way they bend down. Do you know how I usually make beds, for example?" She gave a piece of mime. "That's bound to give me a backache. If you just knew the jobs a woman does all day, lifting things from the floor.

132

It's an awful strain." She demonstrated the television method once again. "This makes a terrific difference," she said. "If I could just get rid of my backaches I'd really do up this cottage."

One of the enthusiasms Ruth never lost was for redecorating. One of her most prized possessions was a blowlamp. Now, in her well-painted kitchen, she began to stare at something which displeased her, something which I couldn't even identify. "I must get on with it," she said. "I've simply got to box off that pipe."

"Have you had a cheer-you-up pill?" I asked her. When she was suddenly bright like this, it sometimes meant that she had taken something. Ruth had a variety of pills. Sometimes she called an aspirin a "fix."

"Yes, one of these delicious mauve ones," she said.

"Why? Because we were arguing about Malcolm?"

"That's right," she said, "but I can't talk about it now. I have to get on with the lunch. It isn't easy here, you know. The food in the shops is pretty basic stuff." She went on about that; the mauve pills were never good for her concentration. She said that tinned foods had been the salvation of these barren lands ever since the Co-op vans had harried, fleet of foot, across the Highland Line.

"I think we should talk about Malcolm and get it over," I said.

"Go on then, talk."

"You don't see that it couldn't have happened, exactly the way Macphail said it did?"

"You said yourself that he was probably telling the truth as he understood it."

"As he understood it, starting off with hating Malcolm. Did you ever see him as a cold killer?"

133

She took a moment to answer and then she said, "No."

"Did you ever know him to go back on a decision, a big decision? When he was younger, I mean, before his confidence was rattled?"

"You're suggesting that it was my fault, that I rattled his confidence?"

"Of course not."

"You sound as if you are. You sound as if you're interrogating me."

"Don't be daft. I'm asking you a simple, ordinary question."

"Well, the answer's 'No.' But I don't know what happened in the Army."

"Now we're getting somewhere. He must have been in a terrible state about something. Something must have happened. He was writing to you every day, I'll bet."

I could remember him sitting in a corner of the mess writing to Ruth. Sometimes he would look up and wink at me when one of the other senior officers refought an old campaign too loudly and ranged us with a word like "Nip," or "woodpecker" for the slow Japanese machine gun.

"You *are* interrogating me," she said. "He didn't talk to you about it. Isn't that some kind of indication?"

"No, he'd had a bellyful of war. He wasn't in the habit of talking about derring-do behind the Japanese lines."

She sat down and put her elbows on the kitchen table, then looked at me with her head cupped in her hands, her soft hair falling over the wrists, her eyes very near and very beautiful.

"You're very loyal to him, aren't you?" she asked.

134

"I don't think the average Watch Committee would see it that way."

"You're very loyal to him. When the times comes, I hope you'll be as loyal to me."

"What do you mean?"

"Oh nothing, women's talk. I started all this and I wish I hadn't now. Don't let's talk about him any more today. What about *us* if we talk about him all the time? What sort of séance would that be?" We dropped it then. It wouldn't have been a good idea to tell her then that I was going to see Dr. Drummond.

The years in London had taken none of the savor from simple things. There was a block and an ax, blond driftwood from the shore which splintered easily. We sat by a dark, slow burn that afternoon and Ruth lay there on her stomach and launched paper boats. On the way to the watershed we were watched from over a dike by deer, looking like large and handsome greyhounds. The sun was hard and hot before we reached the top and the islands in the bay looked near enough to touch. This was one of the few places in Britain where you could make love in the open, in daylight, in the grass, without interesting the police or the trippers.

We went to the pub on that Sabbath night, although we were not *bona fide* travelers. We were not *en route;* we had arrived at our place of destination. The landlord explained this to us while he poured our drinks, on the understanding that we weren't common informers. It was a good night in the pub and we heard Sunndachan (which means Happy Face) McAskill on his best form. He's a local character who makes a summer living from the tourists by running a tea room and claiming a knowledge of fairies. Sunndachan charges fair prices for his teas and nothing for his entertainments. He wasn't exactly a *bona fide* traveler either.

Usually he specializes in fairy dogs and such features of Highland life but, drinking at the public expense that night, he was on about a local hill which he said was called the Hill of Despair. The name suggested literature and the Highland fatalism of Foyles much more than it suggested South Morar, but the tourists seemed quite satisfied.

In the old days, Sunndachan said, cutting black twist into his spoil-hardened hand, neither animal nor bird would cross that hill. It was rumored, right enough, that children had been hidden inside it by the fairies. At night, if you heard a wailing from the hill, you were supposed to take a pail of milk and pour it into the ground, in the center of the fairy ring of stones. When the children had drunk of the milk, the wailing would stop.

He happened to catch my eye at that moment and I nodded solemnly and asked what he would drink. The mountain had moved since the story begun. It was invented in Sutherland in 1943 to keep a certain superstitious gamekeeper off a certain hill when the Home Guard were after the deer. During the war the Home Guard rifle was an excellent provider, but it was reckoned unsporting to go hunting with a Bren gun. . . . Even listening to a Highland fairy story, I had to remind myself of war and Bren guns. We left early.

On the way home Ruth said that she was sorry that she had been "jumpy" that day, that it was all tied up with the feelings she had when she knew, in the night, that something had gone wrong on my visit to Inish.

"I've got two people in the world to worry about," she said, and ran her nails lightly along the back of my hand. "You and Jill."

"Jill's all right, isn't she? She likes staying with your mother?"

"Oh, she's all right. It's just that she's with my mother. I grew up with my mother. It reminds me that she only has one parent, like I had. I want a father for Jill. You like children, don't you?"

"That's a pretty silly question," I said. "I like Jill very much. I like children very much. In my saner moments, I think that life without children is empty and pointless. I get fed up being just an uncle. End message."

"Oh, I'm glad of that," she said. "I'm glad."

12

The outhouse was littered with cracked memories of Ruth's sculpturing period; dirty beige dogs with paws hanging off and pipe-cleaner supports showing through; frightened horses which had never known ears and had been made in a brave attempt to follow Degas.

She had been a writer once, too, and there was a manuscript entitled *A Call on Farthing Mews: By Pagan Dominique*. I remembered the story: it was about a temporary agency typist who had been sent out to work for a young and rising playwright. The children's stories, written in Jill's time, were much better but they were old-fashioned and uncommercial without a pitch-black forest or a beaten-up brownie in them anywhere.

Searching for a hammer, I saw the sack wedged behind an abandoned kitchen dresser, with a metal edge bursting through the jute. It took some time to move the dresser and the sack was very heavy. As soon as I put my hand into it I cut myself. The sack held strange things. There was a Japanese sword, not a Samurai sword, an executioner's weapon. There was a Gurkha *kukri* which didn't look as if it had been used for opening bully-beef tins, a Commando fighting knife and a saw-edged bayonet from an older and more gentlemanly war.

The blades were not as blunt as might have been expected. Someone had kept them sharp through long years of peace. This was an interest which Malcolm had never declared to me. He had despised people who hung weapons or trophies on their walls. In one mess we'd had a leopard, skinned and nailed to the wall like a bat. Malcolm made a point of hanging his keys on its teeth.

From the sack and the wedging position of the dresser I assumed that Ruth had hidden them there after he died. They would be difficult things to leave in a dustbin.

"How did you cut yourself?" she asked, as she bandaged up the hand.

"There was a nail in that last bit of wood," I said, and we left it at that. We were short of time; we had to hurry off to the local hop. She didn't seem to feel like dancing, for once. Usually she danced well and didn't make the customary southern mistake of dancing an eightsome more correctly than the locals. One result was that we were trapped against the refreshment counter by a returned pilgrim from Iona, who traveled through the summer and gave lantern lectures on his travels in the winter.

138

He knew everything about Iona which wasn't worth knowing and I felt sorry for the lecturer's friends who were in for such a long and arduous winter. We would have cut the conversation short but the lecturer had bought us drinks; the lecturer was English and he lingered over his own. I have the fear, common among Scots, of appearing to dodge buying rounds. This has been true ever since a certain comedian became a national hero by teaching the world that the Scots were maudlin and mean.

Ruth refused a cigarette offered by the lecturer when St. Columba was landing in Iona (in A.D. 563) and another offered by the lecturer's wife while her husband was telling a funny story about Iona in a "Highland" whinny, using words like "*ch*entlemen," and "*ch*ust," and "ghostie," which are as exotic in Iona as they are in Manchester. Shortly afterward, we went home.

She changed her clothes to do some job which was never quite defined and by midnight she was sleeping in her chair. She looked graceful, even sleeping in an armchair, and her legs were artistically displayed. She was the only woman I ever knew who could wear a tweed suit and lisle stockings without looking like a recruiting sergeant for the Women's Rural Institutes.

If I covered her with blankets and left her, she'd come into the bedroom at two or three and waken me to complain that I hadn't wakened *her*. If I tried to carry her to bed, she would half-waken on the way and create hell, saying that I was rough and violent. If I woke her, now, gradually, she would be irritable at first, then feel far too refreshed, far too ready to read or talk for the rest of the night or to start some other project. She was always most alive and most ambitious at one and two and three in the morning, after she had slept in a chair. It was at such times that she had written her love stories and become a sculptress. It was at such times she had told me of her readings of philosophy and ended up by saying, "But, anyhow, life is lousy."

Gradually I woke her.

"You ought to have been able to get us to bed hours ago," she said, when she came to. "It's only a question of courage. I'm weak about it; you oughtn't to be weak about it. You ought to be able to get us off to bed. I'll bet Helen made sure that you both got to bed at a proper time." She stretched and looked round for her slippers.

Helen had been reappearing too often in our conversations, but, when Ruth asked about her, precise questions dropped in at unlikely moments, I couldn't sell Helen short; I had to tell the truth about her as I saw it.

"You'll go back to her in the end," Ruth said. "I know you'll go back to her in the end."

This was very unlikely. In the last few weeks I'd found that Helen was a habit which I'd lost and I was pretty certain that Helen felt the same about me.

"I don't think so," I said. "I care for Helen and Helen cares for me just about as much as you cared for Malcolm."

She was coming to then, fast. "You think it was all my fault, don't you?" she asked. "Poor maligned Malcolm. It was all my fault we had a rotten marriage. That's what you think, isn't it?"

"Let's not start on that one," I said. "Let's go to bed."

"Yes, let's go to bed," she said. At half past one she noticed that a piece of the bedroom wallpaper was peeling. It was the damp, Ruth said. Unless she lived in that cottage

140

all year round, she couldn't cope with the damp. Wallpaper never really worked in places like this. When she had time she would strip all of these walls and paint them. Paint would be more suitable for the bothy, anyway.

She tentatively tore at the piece of wallpaper. "See, it's loose, it'll come off easily," she said. "We won't need to use the strippers or anything like that."

"Ruth, for Christ's sake, come to bed." I didn't like the word "we."

"I'll just do this bit," she said. "I just want to see how loose it is. I'll feel happier if I know it'll come off easily." She slid her long fingers behind the loose paper, slowly, rhythmically, searching for the weakness. It was an act of sensuality. "Now," she said, dreamily, gripped tightly and tore. A tattered flag of wallpaper exploded from the wall.

"Please leave it, honey, huh?" I asked. "Just leave it until the morning; I'll help you with it in the morning." At half past two we had both paint strippers at work and the newspapers on the floor were gathering wallpaper and old glue.

She gave up when it was obvious even to her that she wouldn't scrape the entire wall bone clean that night. She sat down beside me and refused a cigarette.

"Malcolm never helped me like that," she said.

"A woman has to like you to make you do things like that."

"It wasn't as simple as that," she said. "When he married me I was seventeen and I thought he was wonderful. But when he came back I had ideas of my own. I couldn't *just* admire him, and that was all he wanted. He couldn't even get that one straight; he couldn't even see that I wasn't in love with him and he wasn't in love with me. Do you know what he once called me? A hedgehog! A small soft

141

thing, covered with bristles, with a remarkably small brain. That was when I didn't treat him as an idol any more. Funny thing about hedgehogs, too. They seem very stupid and unfeeling, but I've heard that hedgehogs scream at night."

"Not only hedgehogs," I said. "Will you *please* come to bed?"

There were twin beds in the spare room. Long after the light was out we lay awake. She was too still to be asleep and her breathing was irregular. She was worrying about something, something more immediate than Malcolm.

"I'd like to come into your bed," I said.

"I like that idea," she said.

"It isn't the old goat again," I said.

"No, I know."

"Just want some kind of contact."

"So do I. Could you kill that cigarette before you move over? It's smoldering somewhere."

She wanted to sleep with her head on my arm, and we lay like that for long enough, while my arm got cramped. After a bit, I made an excuse to turn the bedlamp on. Her face didn't disappear with vanishing cream as some other women's do, and I usually liked to look for the freckles on her eyelids, but she could have used a lot of makeup at that moment.

"Ruth," I said, "I mean, I'm not worried or anything if you are . . . What I mean is, well, I'm with you and we can work this out, and I don't want you to be unhappy about it and, gee-whiz, this sort of thing happens and I'm pretty sure I can get a divorce. It's just that I was stupid not to ask before . . . oh, bloody hell. . . . Are you pregnant?

142

Is that why you aren't smoking and so on?"

She took her head from my arm very quickly and turned away. "Yes," she said after a while. "It's a funny thing to happen, isn't it? I can't stand smoke as soon as I know; it was the same when Jill was coming."

I turned her round when she was shaking something from her nose; she always cried silently. "Don't look," she said. "I can't bear it when you look."

13

I passed the sign which read:

TEAS
Register of Births,
Deaths and Marriages

then I took the track to Dr. Drummond's sheep farm. It was a large farmhouse for Argyll, but the doctor was reputedly rich. He had not practiced since the war. Ruth had gone home to see her doctor and let Jill settle in at home. The arrangement was that I should stooge around for a few more days in the hills. I'd written to Helen. This seemed the time to get the other matter straightened out.

Drummond answered the door himself. He was a long, thin man who held his head forward apologetically, as though he had never rid himself of a schoolboy shame of being tall.

"Cameron," he said. "Come on in. I've heard from Dougal Macphail. Come on in, you're maybe wasting your time, but come on in."

He showed me to a room and to an old chair of light-colored leather by the fire. From the window I could see the last dance of water far off in the heather and the shoulder of a hill which might have been Ben Cruachan. We talked for a bit and then he said, "I've been thinking about this and I don't know that I can help you about Fleming. He was my patient, technically my patient, anyway, and I don't know that I can talk about him. Why do you want to know?"

I tried to tell him, pointing out that I had to get some more sense out of it, understand a bit more, whatever the film company or the survivors might choose to do.

"And where does Mrs. Fleming fit into this?" he asked.

"Oh, we're in it together," I said. "We're . . . we're . . . anyhow, we're in it together."

The doctor grinned. It was a twisted grin. "I'm not surprised," he said.

"What do you mean?"

"I'm asking you the questions at the moment. What did Macphail tell you about it?"

I told him. "Trust Macphail," he said, "a macabre jester, yon. He's given you some of the facts right enough and put a sinister shroud on them. He's a comedian in a great Scottish tradition, the kind of man who makes his best jokes at a funeral." He rose, put another log on the fire and stood watching it.

"If you think that," I began, "and if Malcolm was only technically your patient, don't you think you could—"

"Hold it," he said. "I know where you're driving. But it isn't a simple business of me giving you my version, opening my casebook and the facts leaping out. It's a bit more complicated than that. But if I said that you're right to

144

feel sympathy for Fleming and left it at that, you would go on digging round, wouldn't you?"

"Yes," I said, "and for all I know the film company would do the same."

He ran his hand through his hair. "I don't know what to do about this," he said. "We'll maybe better leave it for a bit. We'll maybe better get on to something else."

He began to talk about the foxes' raids in lambing time and the farmers' reprisals. This theme is obsessive in Highland sheep farmers. When the fox is hunted in the high corries of Argyll there is blood but no sport and no quarter. Like the hill fox himself, the men who hunt him kill often. Anyone who wondered why they kill in such persistence would find their answer in a single fox den, Dr. Drummond said. He had known thirty lambs' heads in one den when it was bolted. Locally, few foxes could find enough hares, rabbits, moles or field mice. They had become delinquent, through environment. Two fox dens, left unmolested when the hills were empty of small game, could easily mean the ruin of a small farmer.

"A clever beast, the fox," Dr. Drummond said.

"Yes," I said.

"There is one fox my men are after tonight," he went on. "Not any fox, a certain fox, one we know too damned well."

"Yes," I said again.

Drummond laughed. "You're determined. And maybe you're better to ask me about it, than to nose about in dustbins. Fire away with your questions," he said.

"You knew him before and after the patrol, after he came home?"

"Yes."

"Did he change much?"

"It depends what you mean by change. Are you one of those lay psychologists? Do you know about the 'subconscious' and the 'inferiority complex' and all the other bits of mumbo-jumbo that no good psychiatrist ever uses?"

"No."

"That's fine; that'll save me going into technical terms. I'm not hellish well up on them myself. Let's put it this way. Fleming changed all the time. I don't know what he was like before the war. But when I first met him he was a damned good infantry officer and playing at being a better one, an iron man." After the patrol, Drummond said, Malcolm came home as a pacifist, a left-wing thinker, a to-hell-with-military-traditions man; the hero turned peace lover . . . his idea of a Second War Siegfried Sassoon. "He was very good at that and, by all accounts, he took you in."

"You didn't like him either."

"I wouldn't say that. Nowadays everything's blamed on the parents, but Malcolm Fleming had pretty strange ones by all accounts. Maybe they should have let him torture a few more frogs when he was small."

"You're saying that he was sadistic?"

The doctor shrugged. He said that he had been brought up on the Moor of Lorn, where life belongs to the quick and to the cunning. The hooded crow would hunt just like the panther, for the hell of it, and peck the eyes out of any ewe if found in difficulty. The fox stole the hooded crow's eggs and the golden eagle killed the crow.

He had known a wild cat caught in a man-made trap to be savaged by foxes before the hunters found it. He

146

took people—like animals—as they were. He did not want to label them.

"But Fleming was a killer, all right," he said, "just as if he'd been a hooded crow. He took you in and he took me in, too, maybe more than once."

"Tell me about that."

"If I told you all about that," he said, "I'd have to give you my own history as well as Fleming's. I'll give you a bit of it though. You have to understand that I fancied my chance as a psychiatrist, once. In fact, I was fancying myself as a head-shrinker on the first morning I ever marched down a hospital ward." Drummond said that he had pins to test reactions in his first long white coat and his stethoscope was round his neck like a feather boa. If he remembered rightly he also had a tuning fork for an extra bit of medical mystique.

By the time he reached Special Forces, he ought to have known better, he said, known how dangerous it was to meddle with the mind. The classic example of what he was driving at was of a man who was "cured" of a hysterical paralysis, convinced that he hadn't got it. The patient committed suicide on the same night.

"But I *didn't* know better, and my first impression of Special Service was that it had a high proportion of head cases, fascinating for me." He would guess that there were also many such in Hitler's S.S.; they fought like people who were sick in the head. "I'm not defining courage on the battlefield as a neurosis, you understand that?" he asked. But he was interested in the theme and he found Fleming fascinating. "At first he seemed so much the conventional show-off soldier," he said. "Show-off?" I asked.

"Oh, yes. He was a real stiff-backed, regimental soldier

147

on detachment when he was with Special Forces; Fleming was always playing a part. Then when he first arrived in the battalion, he was the Special Forces chap with chukka boots and neck scarf, the professional killer bored by all this regimental nonsense. The only thing was that he did the professional-killer stuff too well, as Macphail told you. He would do fantastic things on training, as if he had no sense of fear, as if he'd suddenly switched off."

"And did he have real fear at that time?"

"Oh, God, yes. I'm ashamed to admit it, still, but I had a pretty good idea that Fleming was in a bad way. He would sit for hours staring at something and you would think that it was a great work of art or something, until you found out that he was maybe looking at the label on a bottle of Murree beer. I knew it all belonged to some page of the psychiatry books but I didn't know the page."

Then, he said, there was the incident of the Burmese woman which Macphail had told me about. "What about that?" I asked. "Do you agree with Macphail?"

"I don't know," Dr. Drummond said. "I've heard his version and I've heard Fleming's version." All he could say was that he'd have hated to have been in Fleming's boots at that moment. He was a fighting animal, protecting a whole patrol in sudden danger, in unfriendly country where the Burmese would always "sell us out for two-pence." Time and again in there, gentlemanly behavior was "pretty expensive on British lives." He'd often wondered how Macphail would have reacted in Malcolm's place, if he'd been on his own. "It's often easier to kill than watch a killing," Drummond said. "Did he tell you that Fleming had no knife to make it a quick, clean job? No? Trust Macphail."

When Fleming came to tell him, he said, he didn't seem to appreciate that the interpretation of lies for a doctor was often more useful than a report of symptoms. Fleming said that a friend of his seemed to glory in death in war. Could it be, Fleming asked, that this man was certain of death himself and envied other men their lives?

"I told him that this was one of the more wild theories that I'd heard and that any normal mortal who could hear the trumpets sounding for him on the other side was just as likely to have an awed respect for life, afraid to stand on a beetle," Drummond said. This helped him to steer Malcolm on to talk of his belief that he would die of cancer, a fear he'd had since he was young. "What do you understand by 'cancer,' Mr. Cameron?"

"Oh, I don't know, instead of growing in the normal way, the cells have a sort of wild life of their own . . . they grow at a faster rate, in the wrong direction . . . sort of organic chaos."

"There are worse definitions than that. The surprising thing was that Fleming had *no* definition. 'Cancer' was just something black and horrible of which you died, when you had been tortured for months, and went on being tortured even after the nerves had been cut by a kind surgeon, to ease some of the pain. So much for Fleming's reading and his intelligence," the doctor said. "And he was going to die of it. He had been certain of that since he was young. What did you do about your own fear of cancer, ever?"

"I had a checkup."

"Fleming had no check," the doctor said. "Did you ever hear him speak of Lizzie? A poor woman who came into his house, when he was young, as a charwoman, and became something of a second mother to him, although his

149

mother did not like it?" Drummond said that Lizzie was sacked in the end and that young Malcolm often called on her, without his mother knowing. Then she took ill and he still went round and was still scared that his mother would know. "Lizzie had this . . . whatever it was . . . and she was ill and food tasted like ashes in her mouth and she got to be like a skeleton. Every time young Fleming called, there were people in her kitchen; simple people, not intending to be ghoulish but saying things like, 'It's time she slipped awa'.' 'Maybe the doctor will gie her something painless.' As usual, they assumed that the boy didn't understand a word of it." I grimaced.

"Aye, hellish," the doctor said, "and people never learn." One day, when she was alone, Lizzie polished up her house and, on the mantel shelf, put bundles of money she owed, screwed inside paper and marked in pencil, so much for the rent, so much for the electricity, so much for the milk and rolls, so much for the shoes she was buying on credit. "She wrote a short note to her husband with three misspellings in it and left it on the mantel shelf, too," Drummond said. "And then she took her life."

He had been watching my face and he seemed satisfied with the reaction.

"She couldn't have known that the boy would panic when he found the door closed, on his way back from school," Drummond said. "He was the first to find her. He went out as he came in, through the scullery window, and never told a soul. I'm not surprised you're hissing. I did the same myself, when I heard it, in the jungle."

He began then to try to talk Malcolm away from his fear, night after night. He thought he knew a lot about cancer as well as about minds. Now he knew how little he

150

understood of either. "But I was a great talker in those days," he said.

"Maybe he'd reached the stage when he was ready to shed this fear?" I asked.

"I don't know what you mean by that, but, all right, maybe. What I do know is that I won too easily. My whole medical training told me that was suspect. But I seemed to succeed and the change in Fleming was very, very quick. You know what happened then."

The phone rang and after a bit his housekeeper came in. "It's the fox," she said. "They've got the den and they think the vixen's in it. They've closed it up. The light's too poor to put the dogs in after her and MacDougal has the feeling that the fox might come back and let him have a shot at it when it's light."

"Right, tell him I'll come and relieve him later on and let him get his supper."

"But your chest, your poor chest. Mrs. Drummond said—"

"Mrs. Drummond's on holiday and I'm the doctor here." The housekeeper drew the curtains viciously, half-volleyed at the light switch, then left the room.

"Your face is one big question mark," Dr. Drummond said to me. "Let's have it."

"You want me to be impressed by his fear of cancer but you're not impressed yourself."

He hesitated. "Well," he said, after a moment, "I wasn't, once. I thought his nerve was cracking and this was a fine way to deal with it. I didn't think it was intentional. He thought that Malcolm had probably convinced himself as well as others, but the explanation was altogether too superficial, too glib. Malcolm was suffering from cancerophobia, like millions of other people. But if he got rid of this fear, he would then have good honest motives for being afraid of some other thing. The Japanese, for instance," Drummond said. "It was the same with the other thing he told me, the thing you'll know from Mrs. Fleming about his parents writing to him about her and the Canadian pilot, again."

"Yes?" I said, hoping he'd go on.

"He told me about that, too, later on. It was the wife back home who was costing him his confidence and his courage. At the time I thought I dragged that out of him and then interpreted it. I must have been good and wet behind the ears."

"I'm not sure that I'm following you."

"No, I'm not sure either," Drummond said. "I'm maybe being big-mouthed. The professional habit of discretion has slipped away from me too fast. You'll better ask her about what his parents wrote, and all that."

Drummond seemed to be suggesting that Malcolm had no right to lose courage, no right to be in a poor mental state. He was stripping him of his motives, as if they were epaulettes. I said so and he shrugged.

"If you think that, you've missed the point of all I've told you," he said. "Before we set off, I had a fair idea that Fleming was in no state for the patrol. I could have stopped him going, but I didn't. At the time I thought that I could fix him. It was a simple matter of taking a hammer and a chisel and adjusting a human mind. He broke because he'd been through too much, maybe. If any officer let down that patrol and cost those lives, it was me, not Fleming. It wasn't up to me to have him along as an interesting study. I should have got him off that patrol, as a sick man."

152

"What about the film? Was he sick then?"

Drummond made a spill with a piece of paper from his desk, and folded it very carefully before he put it to the fire. He was deliberate in his movements. He used it, watched it burn down and blew it out when it was an inch from his fingertips.

"I don't know," he said.

Had I ever looked closely at the war-book trade? How many men with something on their consciences had written a book round it, establishing that their consciences were clear, daring their enemies to contradict them? Statesmen, generals, air marshals, war criminals, war crimes judges, they'd all done that. Say Malcolm Fleming had his chance in a film, instead of a book? Say he did defend himself? Why not the humble company commander? No one was attacked in the film according to what Drummond had heard. They were all heroes. The public probably understood more of what that patrol went through from the film than they ever learned from facts.

We were quiet for a while and then I asked him, "Why did you want me to be impressed with all the talk of cancerophobia?"

"Perhaps I wanted to please you. You wanted to believe in Fleming, didn't you? And he wanted you to believe in him. I saw him a few times after the war and that one came across, all right. He wanted you to see his best side. He talked about you often enough." He rose. "I'll give you a lift to the station on the way, but I'll have to go up and relieve MacDougal now. He'll be desperate for his supper."

In his shooting brake, he whistled "The Inverary Inn" and had a conversation with his collie. The discovery of

153

the den and the excuse to visit the hill seemed to be pleasing him.

"After the war, Malcolm got well . . . normal, I mean?"

"Everybody has their own idea of what's normal," Drummond said. "He was all right, maybe, for him. He would rather send someone close to him to the psychiatrist, than go himself. I don't need to underline that, do I?"

On the way, he pointed to the hill where the den had been found and I talked about the beauty of the place. Dr. Drummond said that it had been spoiled for him by certain things found there during lambing; two lambs' heads in the heather, a black cock's feather higher still, very close to a scoop of red earth at the door of the den. The fox had flitted and then come back. "He's getting careless to make his home here again, after that," the doctor said. "Doesn't deserve to survive. Sentenced to death."

A fox would often wander twenty miles in a night, he went on, but he would always come home. They were just like human beings. You would find a grand big lady fox living with a funny little dog fox. You would find dog foxes bringing home "toys" for their cubs to play with—paws, feathers, things of that kind. You would even find peaceable, law-abiding frugal foxes ignoring their bloodthirsty neighbors and living off what rabbits and mice, frogs and beetles they could find. But they all had to suffer for ones like this. . . .

"Dr. Drummond," I said, "you're giving me the idea—and you're not the first—that Malcolm Fleming made a special attempt to impress me, after the war. Why?"

"Yes, I think that's fair."

"But why?"

He hesitated. "One of the things Fleming was afraid of

seems to be happening now. You were one of his great admirers, were you not?"

"Right."

"And he was often afraid that the wife who didn't love him would take you over from him, convert his great disciple?"

"You think it's as simple as that?"

"It could be as simple as that," he said. He stopped, then the thing he had almost said before at last came out. "You'd better know the rest. Fleming died of cancer." I couldn't take that. "Heart failure," I said. I was away, but Ruth told me.

"Cancer," Drummond said. "Cancer made his heart fail."

We were on the main road now. I was numb. In the headlamps, the cats' eyes came up like tracer. "But Ruth said . . ."

"She doesn't know," he said. "I know, I checked up. It was quick, sometimes it's quick. None of his people know. You going to tell her?"

"God, no. But . . ." My questions came in snatches, questions on ticker tape. Who understood how the mind affects the body, how the body affects the mind? Say Malcolm's fear of cancer gave him cancer in the end? Say he pretended to Drummond he was cured, while the fear drove him crazy on patrol? Say his sick body affected his mind, in the film company deal? Or was that all clinical claptrap?

"You tell me," Drummond said. "I failed on those, before. Send your questions on a post card to the Celestial Brains Trust." I tried to light his cigarette, then he threw it away, his mouth was too moist. "Just stop searching, just stop asking people questions," Drummond said.

155

14

Ruth's phone was out of order when I got back to town, so I called round. She was out; the maid said that she wouldn't be back until late that evening. I arranged that she should ring my hotel when she got back, then I took Jill to the toy fair which was being held at the time in the town's largest store. First I had to help Jill bury her goldfish which, she said, had broken its heart while she was away.

The foyer of the store had become a golliwogg's cakewalk but Jill didn't fancy the softer toys. The sophistication of school was beginning to weigh on her and she was only mildly interested in a plastic rocket which could be fired to a hundred feet and which made a noise like a deranged duck. It was reasonably priced, within the range of power maniacs in most school playgrounds. I offered to buy it for her later when I'd drawn some money. She said you went to jail for drawing money.

The next stand held complete sets of soldiers of all nations. Those in United Nations uniform were flanked by another in the ceremonial dress of the Egyptian Army. We passed to the section of children's books. "I like the stories Mummy tells me," she said. "I don't want her to read from a book. When she's telling stories I want to look at her. I like her stories." We walked by.

"Come on," she said. "You'll like this next thing. I know you will. Lot of people there. It must be meant for grownups."

156

"Look at that plastic egg," the salesman said. "Absolutely lifelike, isn't it? Two or three months' waiting list for joke eggs, now. See this? Stick it on your head and it looks like a boil. Absolutely perfect, isn't it? Next item . . . imitation blood."

We began to move away, before the blood was demonstrated, just as a customer demanded, "Any of that stuff? Put it on the carpet or a cushion. Looks like human dung?"

"None of that," the salesman said coldly. "That's a foreign patent. Nothing but good taste on this stand."

Then we were lost among World War III accessories. The absence of germ warfare kits or boys' brain washing outfits showed either a certain lack of initiative or the fast-changing fashions of war. "Oh, look," Jill said, "look at that." She was seeing between adults and she had to guide me to the makeup sets for small girls and companion make-up sets for their dolls.

"I'm glad we found that," Jill said when we left the fair. "Nearly everything seemed to be for boys. I'm glad. I have to go home now and show this to my dolls. Everything else was for boys, really. I hope the baby in Mummy's tummy is a boy, much more things for boys to buy." I tried not to tighten my grip on her hand.

"Who told you about that?"

"Oh, my grandmother," she said, "but she said it was a secret."

In the evening I hung around a bar of the hotel, waiting for Ruth to ring. For company I had Joe Duncan and the barman, who was on about the weather. He was convinced that it was the hydrogen bombs that did it. The barman said that we shouldn't listen to the denials of the scientists; that was all part of the sinister conspiracy to keep the truth

157

from us. He'd had a bit of proof of unnatural weather during the last summer tornado—a hailstone as big as a brick. He put it in the fridge to show to the men from the newspapers. The only snag was that the storm that brought the hailstone also played hell with the electricity and cut off his fridge.

Joe didn't hold with the theory. He said that he'd felt much safer in his bed ever since we started setting off hydrogen bombs of our own. He also said that he was waiting for somebody. From school days, Joe had been waiting for someone. He had a deep, secret well of optimism.

"Will there be more people in later on?" I asked him, when the barman had finished his talk on the weather, ending with the theory of his uncle's that it was all the good air trapped in pneumatic tires that had brought about a change of climate. The barman didn't think much of that.

"Maybe," Joe said, "maybe. Buzzing with life, isn't it? Come to Bonnie Scotland for a rest cure."

"You could see it that way," I said, "but I like it quiet here. I used to feel the way you do. Maybe that's why I went to London. But I don't know, now. It's maybe better like this. London's too restless, too many people determined to enjoy themselves, making themselves miserable trying to enjoy themselves." I could see that I wasn't convincing him. "In the belt I live in," I said, "they even go in for wife-swapping parties."

Joe exchanged a glance with the barman. "That's terrible," the barman said. "That London's a terrible place."

"Shocking," Joe said. "Are you doing anything this evening, Tom? That's a pity. I could have shown you something. One of the few places in town where I'm really welcome. And you'd have been welcome, too. They're always looking for new talent. I'm afraid you'd never meet Mrs. Fleming there, though." News travels fast in our town.

He began to discuss the wife-swapping parties held locally, in such unloving detail that he might have been talking about the Stephenses' set of Sidney Court, South Chelsea. Here too they put cushions in front of the lampshades and danced to the music of combined television sets, radios and tape recorders so vast and menacing that they looked like electronic brains.

The play room of one house he described even sounded like the Stephenses' main room, which was in what they were pleased to call Regency style and which, remarkably, had incorporated so many of the less fortunate features of the Royal Pavilion without any of the sense of color or design. Here, too, they had the tape-recorder joke: microphones were hidden in bedrooms and the recording played back to the whole party.

"But how do they get away with it here?" I asked. "The town's so small. I would have thought that after six months of that stuff, there would be so much gossip and slander that they'd have to convene a mass divorce trial."

"Don't you believe it," Joe said. "The lord provost's wife and the chief constable's wife are in on it. Couldn't be safer than if it was run by Nero." He said that some of what he called the "stock" were assembling at that very moment in the hotel's Braemar Cocktail Lounge. "Come on, I'll introduce you," Joe said. "You need convincing."

"I'll take your word for it."

"Come on, come on. It'll be good for your education. Living in London's made you narrow-minded."

The group he brought me to in the Braemar Cocktail Lounge drank slowly and talked quietly but, in the hotels of our town, only strangers ever behaved in any other way. Loud talkers and fast drinkers belonged in pubs. Their quiet talk was just as brittle, facetious and laden with ponderous innuendo as it would have been at the Stephenses'. One man said that another man's wife was looking younger every day and the husband replied, "I know, she ought to be in a gym slip. What's the secret, dear? Stuffing your glands with wheat germ?"

The wives were very intense. I don't suppose their husband-swapping activity arose as much from sexual as from emotional frustration. They knew and read of grand raging passions and they knew that their own husbands were only shot with emotion when they were talking about stag hunting or bus drivers who ignored them at request stops.

A candle-faced man in a tired dinner jacket was being badgered by one of the women. "What were you writing down in your diary?" she asked.

"The round of drinks I've just bought."

"A note of your expenses, chargeable to income tax? You mean the tax inspector looks on us as business contacts?"

"I don't know," he said. "Don't pry into my affairs."

"I'm not prying. I'm asking a simple, straightforward—"

Just as I was about to leave, a small, large-breasted woman who was blonde and as watchful as a seagull was introduced as a doctor's wife. She seemed to know my name and she said that I should have brought Ruth with me.

"Oh, she's busy," I said, "got a lot of things to do." She was smiling in what I assumed was a patronizing way and I added, "And she isn't very well."

160

"Oh, you've nothing to worry about," the doctor's wife said. "She'll be all right. I'm not saying she's a hypochondriac. Don't think that for a minute. But she's nervous, you know, highly strung, easily worried. When Malcolm was alive she kept imagining she was pregnant."

15

Ruth rang about an hour later and we went to the pub we had first used together, the pub out of town on the river, which still had seats made from beer barrels, chatty handouts on the vintage years for wine, and wickerwork baskets full of dog biscuits on the tables. It was the only place in the area with a regular late license. You could drink if you ate. We had trouble with the menu. Some innocent Scottish dishes sound sinister in French.

"Well, talk about it," Ruth said. "All those automatic answers and all the time you're looking at me like that, like you were trying to memorize my face. What is it? Is it about us or Malcolm or what?"

While I went over some of what Drummond had said, I had trouble with my hands. When I can't get words out I try to shake them out with my hands. I ended with them in my pockets, asking, "What about this fear of cancer, then?"

"I suppose he feared it," she said. "Yes, he feared it."

"Funny you never mentioned it."

"Is it? He was afraid of lightning, too. It would take weeks to tell you all the things that Malcolm feared."

161

"What about the Canadian pilot? Was that the one you knew before?"

"You believe that?" she asked. "You believe that just like Malcolm's parents did when they wrote to him? You believe that, like he believed it?"

"I asked you what might be worrying him," I said, "and you didn't know. You didn't know about the letters his parents wrote, just like you didn't know about the cancerophobia?" I didn't want to play the interrogator, but I couldn't find a gentler set of words.

"You're calling me a liar, aren't you?" she asked. "You're calling me a liar."

"No, I'm not calling you a liar. Maybe you don't know where truth ends and what you want to believe begins." She looked down at the tablecloth then and began to draw rings on it with a finger.

"Thank you," she said. "Thanks very much. I wouldn't have thought my father-in-law making a fool of himself was the truth you'd want to know."

The car park lay beyond our window and somebody out there was fiddling with a radio. The tune was familiar Lonnie Donegan and so were the words,

Putting on the agony, putting on the style,
That's what all the young folks are doing all the while.

The wine waiter came back and he held the bottle label forward, so close that he must have thought I followed Braille with my nose. I nodded, he poured a little in my glass and stepped back, as if he had performed a conjuring trick. "Please, just pour it," I said. He looked hurt, poured as for lemonade, and went.

"And?" Ruth asked. "That's not all, is it? What comes next?"

"The film company. They had to hush this business up, didn't they? At the start they told you that they could hush it up? You were pretty quick to mention it when I came back from Macphail. It just struck me—I must have been pretty dumb for it not to strike me before."

The radio tune had changed; now somebody was singing,

Times are get-ting hard, boys, mon-ey's get-ting
scarce,
If things don't get much bet-ter, boys, I'm gon-na
leave this place.

Ruth said, "Yes, all right, I'll take the point about the film company. I'll accept that."

"Why?" She didn't answer.

"Why?" She shook her head.

"Not difficult to work out, is it, Ruth? You and I were together again and I was still hellish guilty about Malcolm, more worried about 'disloyalty' to a dead friend than to a live wife. So I had to find out what he was like for myself? I had to tear him down with my own hands?" The radio played,

But all that I can of-fer you is my un-dying love.

"That's right," Ruth said, "that's right. I didn't think you'd take it so hard. I thought you'd have given up earlier. I thought it was the easy way out. I was living with you and I couldn't get close, not really close. You were still hanging on to . . . this cardboard picture of Malcolm. I had to get it away from you. It was in the way. I had to get rid of it. What was so terrible about that?"

The radio was switched off when the car started. The people at the next table had stopped talking. It turned out

163

that the woman was considerately silent, while the man looked at the bill.

"Why didn't you just tell me yourself?" I asked.

"Tell you about *him*? You wouldn't have believed me. He was your hero, wasn't he? Have you ever thought out *why* he worked so hard to be your hero?"

"Drummond told me. That makes me feel like a bloody slug. Why was that another thing you didn't tell me about?" She didn't answer straightaway because the food arrived. We prospected with forks for a bit, then she pushed her plate away.

"How much do you want to know about Malcolm?" she asked. "I tried to make it easy. How much do you need to know before you feel you haven't got to erect a permanent spiritual monument to his memory? Do you want to know about our sex life or his atrocity pictures? Do you want to know about his Mussolini set?"

"For Christ's sake," I said.

"Shut up, shut up and listen. He had just about every picture of Mussolini hanging upside down like a piece of bleeding meat, in that market square in Milan. I used to have nightmares about that face, upside down and the blood running and the eyes popping out. He liked to show me those pictures. They used to give me nightmares."

Her face was so tight that lines appeared above her cheekbones, like pink, inaccurately drawn extensions of an eyebrow line, if she had painted her eyebrows. She didn't paint her eyebrows.

"Have I got a smut on my face or something?" she asked.

"No."

"If I *have* got a smut on my face I wish you'd tell me."

"You haven't got a smut on your face."

"Often when I have a smut on my face you don't tell me."

"Because I don't notice."

"Because you don't notice. There isn't anything about you I don't notice."

"Where's this taking us?"

"Back to Malcolm, something you're interested in. The one thing about me which always interested you was that I was married to Malcolm. When he was alive, that was all we ever talked about, even when we were on our own. Malcolm. And there were always so many things I couldn't tell you about Malcolm."

The plates were taken away and the coffee came. It was Nescafé or Maxwell House, solemnly served.

"So much," she said again, "and now you want to know. I haven't been fair, I haven't told you enough. Do you want to hear about our sex life?"

"No."

"He didn't like it, unless it was right after a row. And he made some marvelous rows. Did you know that I once had a tooth on a dental plate?"

"Steady up," I said.

"What's the point of steadying up now? He was needling me, needling me this night, and I wouldn't provoke. I had this tooth on a dental plate. It's bridged now. I don't think about it now. I haven't got any feeling about it, one way or the other. But when I first had this plate in my mouth, I was very selfconscious about it. It made me aware of the skull under my face. It was, I don't know, decay, the first sign of the body going to rot. Sometimes I would suddenly remember about that plate when I was

165

talking to somebody and it would feel so large and awkward, like I was chewing celluloid. And I was talking this night, trying to keep calm, when he suddenly reached out and took the dental plate from my mouth. I started to cry and that made him feel peaceful, made him feel strong. He held the plate by the metal band and he dried it all with his handkerchief and he handed back the plate. About half an hour after that, he began to make his pass; he always liked to fight for it. If the noise wakened Jill, he'd send her back to bed and put a chair against our door. A chair. There were no locks, remember? Stop whistling under your breath. Listen, *listen*. Don't try to close your mind to this." I hadn't been aware of whistling. It was the first tune,

Putting on the agony, putting on the style,
That's what all the young folks are doing all the while.

"Sometimes I would give in," she said. "Sometimes, just to get it over. After that he would talk about what it had been like, how rotten and frustrating it all was. Then he would go on at me, talking about how mad I was—one of us had to be nuts, he could see that all right. Did you and Helen ever fight, really fight?"

"Yes."

"Have violent fights, physical fights?"

I said yes, but the answer was no. Sometimes Helen would throw something into the fire but she always seemed compelled to throw crockery which was old and chipped, or from sets in which items could be replaced.

"Did you ever argue about *me* in the middle of the night?"

"You? No."

166

"That was the way Malcolm provoked me into rowing," she said, "talking about you. Know what he called you? My phantom lover. On and on and on, questioning me about you, about the times we were supposed to meet in secret. Every time I went to my mother's, he rang up with some phony excuse to check up that I was there. And he checked on you, how he checked on you. And you never knew."

"No."

"You mean you don't believe me?"

"Oh, I believe you." This fitted into the puzzle exactly. He often asked me about somewhere I'd been, months after I'd told him. At the time I thought he was only forgetful.

Ruth talked on. " 'Where were you?' he would ask when I got home, as if he didn't know, as if he hadn't checked. 'Were you with your phantom lover? How did you do it? Standing up? Does he know the things you like? Does he know all the things I know?' And once he got me crying or throwing things at him, he made a pass, he made another pass."

She usually talked from deep down, with no throat constriction, no unnecessary interference. Somebody, sometime, had taught her about relaxing or how to give the impression of relaxing. Now her voice was higher, fast and flat, the words queuing up and struggling through the crush.

"And Jill came into that," she said. "Jill was your child, according to Malcolm, when he really got worked up; your child, didn't you know? That was why you were so warm with her. He even worked out the dates to suit a couple of nights I spent in London."

"He must have been . . . upset."

"Mad? Oh, yes, maybe. And cunning enough in the way he handled you to be really mad. Maybe we're all mad. Maybe madness is the excuse for anything. Every bloody lapsed Christian that I know has his own personal vision of Freud. I can see it in your face. All right, I hated him, I hated him and I'm bloody glad he's dead. Let's go."

She took the cigarette. "The first morning after we were married," she said, "I can remember that. Malcolm didn't smoke, didn't mind me smoking of course, just didn't smoke himself. In bed the night before I told him all about the Canadian pilot . . . all there was, there was never any more, all before his time. He didn't say anything. Just, the next morning things had changed. When I woke up, he'd been out and bought himself some of these bloody awful Turkish cigarettes they had in all the shops those days. He came over to the bed, smoking one of these things, and blew it into my face. All he wanted to do, he said, was to let me know what it felt like to have tobacco smoke in your face. He just wanted me to try to stop. Never mentioned the Canadian pilot."

"You should have told me all this before."

"Should I?" she asked. "Should I? I wonder. Get that bill and let's go."

It was quiet outside the pub, so quiet that we heard an owl scream and fall on something soft. It was dark, so dark that the hills seemed very high against the night. The car was alone in the park. "Where do you want to go?" she asked.

"For a walk along the cliffs?" I asked. She nodded, started up and drove off. "Why didn't you leave him?" I asked.

"Wondered when you would ask that." She talked very quietly and the engine was noisy and I got the sense rather than the words. She wasn't certain why she hadn't left him. Was it because if you were the child of a broken marriage yourself, you would go through most things to make the marriage work; go on until you didn't have the energy to leave; go on unless he tried putting rat poison in the tea? Was it because she thought he was sick and you just didn't get up and leave people, especially people who were sick in the head; not because you felt genuine sympathy but because you thought of yourself and thought that leaving sick people was despicable?

"And then there was Jill," she said, "and she adored him —he handled her just like he handled you. Why didn't I leave him? You choose."

"I'm not very good at choosing," I said.

We got out and walked along the cliffs. The wind was coming up and over it the moon was riding high and clear, like a canoe, with hardly a splash of cloud across its bow. She had a graceful, easy, silent walk and the moon was bright on her hair. Then she stumbled. "I'd better be careful," Ruth said. "If I fell here, after they saw us arguing in the pub, in the circumstances, you'd have a lot of explaining to do."

She made me feel strange, she was so calm, so persuasive when she talked like that. I had wanted to say this without being clumsy but I muffed it. "Ruth, I know you're not having a baby," I said.

She stopped and began to cry then. When she really cried, she made a noise, a harsh noise. I tried to put an arm round her shoulder, but she pushed me off with the arm strength of a man. "I didn't reckon on that," she said.

169

"I didn't reckon on that being part of your detective work."

"I know you made a mistake," I said. "I know you thought that—"

"Shut up," she said, "just shut up."

I waited, handed her a handkerchief, then took it back quickly. The handkerchief had been used at the funeral of Jill's goldfish. Jill hadn't cared for the fish in life. In death, it had a special significance and it was now sleeping for ever in her window box.

Ruth stood crying and she shivered once and I gave her my jacket. "You knew and you kept quiet?" she said. "I was going to tell you, didn't know how to tell you, and you knew, you were just listening and waiting, coldly? You must hate me, you really must."

"Oh, I don't hate you. You fascinate me; you always will."

She gave me my jacket back. "That isn't quite the prettiest speech you ever made," she said.

"If you won't wear my jacket, let's go and sit in the car."

"If you mean sit in the car," she said. We went back and sat in silence. There was an inside light and she tried to use it, tried to look at her face in the driving mirror. "You said you weren't good at choosing," she said, "but you are, you know. You're good at choosing to run. You always run away from unhappiness, don't you? And I've been fairly clanging away with the leper's bell. I wasn't going to spoof you about the child; honestly, I wasn't. I just thought, give it a few more days, give it time. . . . But you don't think it would work. Don't deny it; you're frightened of the whole thing now, you want to run."

It was a flat statement; she didn't want a reply. I said

170

nothing but I must have whistled under my breath again
for she began to sing, tunelessly, ironically,

Putting on the agony, putting on the style,
That's what all the young folks are doing all the while.

"Do you hate me?" she asked again.

"God, no, why would I hate you? I'll always wonder
what's happening to you, where you are, who you're with,
what you're thinking about." I knew it would be like that.

"And you'll go back to your wife."

"No." Even if I wanted to, even if she wanted me, I
couldn't go back to Helen and say, "Please, miss, it was all
the other woman's fault. Please, miss, I was in love but it
didn't work out. Please, miss, will you darn my socks
again?"

Ruth switched off the inside light. "You're a funny
character," she said. "I ought to hate you, now, but I don't.
I hope you won't be lonely . . . in London."

I thought of having a small flat . . . in Chelsea, then I
was aware of the Sidney Court complex that implied, the
desire to escape from life, which was Sidney Court, to
Chelsea which was the nearest landfall of the continent
of fantasy.

Central London didn't have air like this, space like this.
It didn't give me any of the sense of belonging which I
sometimes felt here. But it didn't need to be lonely. However woolly your ideas were, however indecisive you
were, you'd always find a soul mate there. It was large
enough for the doubters, the faithless, the morally under-
privileged. You could run away forever and still stay in
London. It was a Casbah for the likes of us.

"I want you to stay," Ruth suddenly said. "I want you to

171

stay. I want you to forget about Malcolm. I want you to forget about the . . . tricks . . . I played on you. I want you to stay and see how it turns out."

"I'm due back on the twentieth," I said. "I think, well . . . maybe better not. This is crazy. We can't start from scratch. If we were just meeting now, no ghosts, no memories to share . . . That's what *you* want to do. Start from scratch with somebody."

We sat there until we were cold, until the stars were hard and bright, and the wind was tearing at the hood.

"Will you drive?" she said.

I started up, engaged gear and the wheels slid. We were bogged; we had stayed too long on the soft ground beyond the cliff. I tried reverse and the same thing happened. "We need branches," I said, "under the back wheels, lots of them. I'll get them if you'll wait."

When the pine branches were piled, she insisted that I drive while she stayed outside to guide me. For a moment nothing happened and she was standing there, beckoning me, compelling me in the blaze of the headlamps. Suddenly the wheels gripped, the car shot toward her and she fell.

As I braked, my first reaction was *if she's dead it will look like murder* and then I was out of the car, shouting, "Ruth, Ruth."

She still lay on the ground and I ran to her, then I stopped. She was clear in the head lamps and too perfectly arranged. The angle was odd. I had to look at the tire marks; then I was certain that the car had not struck her.

I considered all this coldly before I said, "That was awful. Did I hit you?" Then I began to laugh. It was the

172

sudden relief of tension; I didn't mean to laugh; I didn't find the situation very funny.

16

I went over the zebra crossing outside our studios like an engineer walking away from a demolition charge, neither running nor walking, eyes fixed firmly in front. This crossing had obviously been planned by the undertakers in collusion with the road-accident statisticians and the brake-lining manufacturers. Since I left the car with Helen I had become a hardened pedestrian, but my feet were sore.

In the lift, I thought of larger problems. I had come back to London, determined to make a go of the divorce series, working with a happily married Catholic director to ensure a balance of prejudice. But in the whole of our department there was one light and efficient sound camera which we needed, a camera which wasn't cumbersome and which didn't look like the central feature of a camel train when it was on the move. I couldn't have that camera for at least a month. There was a spare which might have done but it was held against dire emergencies, such as a lightning strike at the B.B.C. That's television. An American producer said that crisis is the backbone of the film industry, that they are only truly stimulated by hysteria. In British television, our inspiration is frustration. There is never more than one battery for the idiot lantern and the battery is always low. But I was researching, beavering away at nights at my flat, in the undisputed land between Earls Court and Fulham, far from Chelsea.

The liftman and a friend were talking about a budgereegah which had been left by an open window while it was molting, and which had died of flu. The man who did that ought to be struck off the club membership, they agreed. The liftman noticed that I was listening and turned to more usual aspects of his hobby. It turned out that he had a budgereegah called Phyllis and she was azure blue.

I was reminded that flu, even flu for budgereegahs, meant that the summer was almost over. In Battersea Park, the boats would have lost the color of summer; there would sometimes be a light mist on the pond, a darker gray in the swirling papers and a new hungry stridency in the dirty ducks, deprived of summer bread. I hadn't been to the flat; so far as I knew Helen had let it. But soon, too soon, the plane trees beyond it would be scruffy.

My secretary was in the cubicle which is called an office and, laughably, has a separate inventory. "Morning, Maureen. Anyone ring up?" I asked, still hopeful about the camera.

"They're running an old film on divorce through for you," she said, "dubbing theatre after lunch. Sorry if I woke you too early." When I did not show up by eleven, she always rang my flat. She was a plain, helpful girl with husband trouble.

"No, you didn't, thanks a lot," I said. "How's the research?"

While we waited for the camera, she was wading through the evidence offered to the Royal Commission on Marriage and Divorce. We were impressed by the superb weight of statistical claptrap, offered as "evidence"

174

by interested parties, each set of figures canceling out the last.

"This isn't bad," she said, and handed me over a sheet which read,

Quote: *We do not see that a divorce between fact and law is a good thing.*

Quote: *The Law cannot make people love each other and it cannot make them live together if they do not choose to do so.*

Quote: *Where in the Gospel is a message warning us to restrain our sympathy for individual cases?*

Quote: *Claims for damages should be abolished absolutely. Such actions merely serve to put a monetary value on a wife and bring her to the level of cattle being priced and sold in a market.*

"There's another one, but I've lost it," Maureen said. "One dear old judge asked a Church witness why the courts should try to stop Church members from divorcing. 'Wasn't that the Church's job?' he asked . . . or something like that."

I sat down, picked up a pencil, then dropped it. She never let me doodle on a clean blotter. "Maureen, I'm with you, all the way. But we're supposed to be preparing an impartial series of programs, not an attack on the law, and on privileged opinion. Let's have the other side."

She shrugged, opened the drawer of her typing desk and produced another sheet.

Quote: *What therefore God hath joined together let no man put asunder. Nothing but death can sever the bond of valid, consummated marriage between Christians. There are indeed hard cases. . . . Christ knew every single "hard case" that would exist to the end of time.*

I asked her to mark up all the best Church quotations, in favor and against relaxing the law. Whatever we achieved in this course of the series would have to end with a studio discussion in which Christian opinion—of some kind—would triumph.

"Anything else?" I asked.

"Nothing much. Did you know that there were seventy thousand separated wives on national assistance and twenty thousand of them over sixty, when this came out?"

"I can well believe it."

"And one newspaper claims to have proved that most marriages break up on the weekends?"

"I can vouch for that, in person. Anything else?"

"Just this." She handed me the sheet which read,

Quote: *When you are listening to fifteen years of married life potted by the parties to an afternoon, who can say who drove the wife to nag or whether she is a nagger by nature?*

"I would send that to my husband . . . if I just knew where he was," Maureen said.

"No news of him?"

"No, but I think there's news of your wife," she said. When I didn't reply, she turned to her typewriter, opened her shorthand notebook, put a sheet of headed paper and two copies into the machine and began to type. This would have been impressive if I'd dictated anything to her recently. "All right," I said, "let's have it." I'd heard nothing of Helen. She hadn't even replied to my letter from the cottage near Arisaig.

"I don't know, I just think," she said. "I heard Willie Greenhill and Sam Winters talking. You know how men gossip when there aren't any women around? I heard them mentioning your wife's name but I couldn't make it out. They shut up when they saw me."

176

Sam wasn't on until three and I couldn't reach him by phone. I tried the studio club for Willie and for the first ten minutes I was stuck with our most terrifying quiz kid, who insisted on telling me the names of every woman executed in the last forty years. She had suddenly remembered; it was an odd trick of memory, she said. She'd been known to do this on a program. Her specialty was ancient British traditions such as "Where is Shrike Friday celebrated?" and "What is the origin of Wuppity Scoorie on skates?"

I saw Willie, excused myself at murderess Edith Thompson, and walked across. He was with a group of young actresses but eventually they were escorted out by a bored agent who had been showing them round with all the brisk and impressive inefficiency of a restaurant car waiter.

"Have you seen anything of Helen?" I asked Willie.

"Me? Let me think. No," he said.

"You're a producer. Nobody would ever hire you as an actor. Where was it, at the Stephenses'?"

Willie was indignant. "I just heard about her, that's all. And yes, it was at the Stephenses'. I was doing some more research for *The Small Gilded Fly.*"

"Willie, I know you were. I'm not questioning your morals. What did they say about Helen? It's all over. You can tell me."

He told me that Helen was going to marry someone I knew well, someone I thought would suit her. I should have known about that man; he wasn't a bad choice either; I should have known about that a long time before.

I went to the dubbing theatre, where films are shown and a commentary added, where lengths of unfortunate or uninteresting truth are hacked and slashed in the interests

177

of entertainment. There I had to wait before my film was shown. There was another man ahead of me, preparing a program called "The Fifties." As a serious offering to preserve the balance of programs, it was naturally made up cheaply; chiefly from old newsreel film.

The producer had almost an embarrassment of interesting wars in the fifties from which he could choose. There were shots of Russian tanks in Budapest, French paratroopers in the Casbah; death in Poland, Egypt, Cyprus, Kenya and Korea. Peace between the nations was not overlooked and there were handshakes by flashlight in Downing Street, ticker tape parades in New York, one short take of Marshal Tito in Abyssinia and one of Mr. Malenkov in Britain, talking to the Dagenham Girl Pipers' band. The death of Stalin was given at the same length as the wild scenes when the last exhausted London tram car crossed the Thames.

At 2:59 precisely I left the theatre and made the corridor between the lift and Sam's office. "Tom," Sam said, in greeting, coming up from behind. As he came alongside, he surreptitiously changed step to keep things tidy and we marched thereafter at his regulation 160 paces to the minute, with the point of Sam's umbrella beating out the time.

"Lot to get through before we line up cameras," he said, looking up at the electric corridor clock and checking it against his watch.

"Peasants," Sam said. "That clock's slow. They'll adjust before we go on the air. Bound to adjust before we go on," he went on. "Imagine being half a minute out. Imagine." His wife swore that if he got into his bath and found that the soap was missing, he would wash with foaming

178

cleanser if he was making an attempt to smash his record over the distance.

I asked him about the man Helen would probably marry and he said that he didn't even know the name.

"Let's save the delicacy," I said. "It's all right. I don't want to fight a duel or anything. Just tell me how long this has been going on. I just want to know, plain curiosity." He told me and it turned out that it had been in full swing long before our final row, long before I went to Scotland. In time of trouble, they met at the Stephenses'. I thought of all the pointless arguments we'd had. I would never understand women.

"How's your divorce series going?" he asked, guardedly. Since I'd come back, Sam was beginning to suspect me of sincerity. He didn't see that I couldn't go on as before. Living with Ruth, finding out about her and Malcolm and myself, I found that I had no standards by which to judge his actions, hers or my own. I had to look around for a set of values. My long postwar time of searching round for something to disbelieve and something to be contemptuous about had to end. "Television," Sam said, "the swamp of fools. It sucks down everybody in the end."

After the film I wrote a letter to Helen, a business letter, suggesting that we wind things up. It was almost as difficult as the divorce letter and I was still on it, on the following afternoon, when the call came through from Scotland.

At first I thought it was from Ruth and there was no good reason why I should be so pleased to hear from Ruth. It was Fergus Macdonald, from the regimental depot.

"I've been trying to get in touch with you all over the place," he said.

"If it's general mobilization," I said, "I know a place in Mull where I can hide."

"Colonel Humphries wants to see you. He's in town, at his club. Will you ring him there? Will you, Tom? Very important. This is your big chance to get me out of trouble and even up the score."

"What do you mean, even up the score?"

"Come off it, the time you lost your bearings on field firing in the bush and emptied a whole bloody magazine of Bren bullets over the brigadier's head. Who got you out of that? Who hid the cartridge cases? Me."

"What kind of trouble are you in?"

"I think you can guess. See you soon," he said, and rang off.

It was best to get it over with, straightaway, so I rang Humphries at his club and arranged to meet him for tea.

It would be something to do with Malcolm and I didn't want to distress or distract the old boy. I was wearing a dark gray suit with suède shoes, a semi-obligatory uniform for documentary producers. The shoes would not do. I put on the black shoes which had been in my locker ever since a Very Important Person visited the studios and paraded at his club, precisely on the minute he had suggested. At that minute, when it was far too late, I realized that I was wearing green socks. Fortunately, his was one of the smaller, hearty, leathery clubs, not one of the drained and silenced swimming baths.

In civilian clothes Colonel Humphries looked less than middle height and slightly shabby. It had not occurred to me before that he lived on his pay or that the Army, his whole life, had denied him promotion and fulfillment. He must have been close to the age for retirement and I could see him taking a house close to the depot and coming in for regimental dinners and retreats. It wasn't much of a prospect. It was strange to feel sympathy for Humphries, especially while he was talking. I hadn't known that he had a son on the stage, or that his wife kept a guinea pig called Billie, or that his youngest daughter did the football pools and put a cross in one corner to ensure anonymity when she won. People are funny.

I'd had only one moment of sympathy for Humphries in the past. He had been talking about what a good idea it would be to send touring cricket and rugby teams of public schoolboys round the Welsh coalfields in this brave new world of 1945. He'd said that the schoolboys wouldn't mind. Malcolm had interrupted. He had pointed out that the miners would mind slumming very much indeed. Humphries had gone white, thanked him, and said that he hadn't thought of that.

"Let's get to the point, then," Humphries said. "You'll have gathered that I've found out about your investigations? Your jump behind that weapon store was clumsy, Cameron. Captain Macdonald and Sergeant-Major Sampson are far more easy to handle than they used to be. You've spoken to Macphail?"

"And Dr. Drummond, sir. It isn't a black and white case of cowardice. It isn't anything simple."

He was smiling. "My dear Cameron, there's no need to be heated," he said. "I never saw it as a 'black and white case of cowardice.' I never saw it as anything 'simple.' I knew most of the facts you know now, quite a long time ago." He said that it was up to the regiment to protect Fleming, that he had tried to explain that to him, at the time. He tried to tell Malcolm that he alone was in a position to judge whether they should have retreated when they were ambushed, that he alone could decide whether

181

it was wise to split the patrol and send the weaker and slower men on ahead. "So that they could rendezvous further west . . . and be together at the point where most Japanese opposition was to be expected." Humphries emphasized his words. "He alone could judge whether he could save Ramsay after that second, wholly unlucky ambush. Personally I think he was right not to try. I think it would have ended with them all in the bag."

"You're sure he intended to rendezvous further west, sir?"

"The evidence suggested it."

"Drummond didn't know that."

"So far as I know, Drummond didn't ask. He didn't come back to the battalion, you know."

"But when he left on his last walk, Ramsay said he'd have Malcolm court-martialed, he said that—"

"Ramsay was a hothead, like yourself," the colonel said. He hoped that he hadn't been wasting my time but he wanted to make sure that I hadn't taken Sergeant-Major Sampson's or Captain Macdonald's word for it. They had misunderstood his reasons for demanding silence. Colonel Humphries would not have any more ill-informed gossip. He wanted me to know that Fleming had asked for a court-martial and that the regiment had blocked it. . . .

He stopped talking for a minute and looked across at the elderly men in one corner who seemed unable to believe the outcome of a horse race on the television screen.

"I'm afraid I wasn't very understanding, Cameron, when Fleming came back. I talked about the blocked court-martial and made some very bitter remarks about him having asked for one. After that he cut me. I didn't try very hard to understand individuals. I wanted everyone

to fit into the pattern. Thank you for your loyalty to
Fleming. Any man can have bad moments and he was
entitled to his."

He seemed to be implying that I could keep my hero.
I hope I sounded grateful enough. The depth of my disloyalty to Malcolm was beyond, below the Colonel's understanding.

At the end Humphries, of all people, was the charitable
one. Humphries of all involved was the one to come out
with credit, with drums beating and bayonets fixed.

He cut and spread some bread with precision. "Let's
have this taken over to the television set," he said. "I think
that's the 4:30 beginning now."

17

Helen phoned. We had to get organized, she
agreed, go over the gear we had and split it down the
middle. Of all places, we met at our old flat.

It wasn't easy to work out who owned what but we did
our best and we touched on the subject of a divorce.
After all the stuff Maureen had dug up, I knew some of
the pitfalls we had to avoid. When I left, I said I was
going to walk through the park.

"I think I'll come," Helen said. "We never did look at
the funfair together. And we talked about it for years and
years."

We walked along the river walk for a bit, sometimes
looking down at the shudder of tide in the water, admiring
the shooting-gallery stagger of lights on Albert Bridge.

Then we went an avenue deeper into the park, when the funfair was almost closing.

Beyond it the lights were going out in Prince of Wales Drive and Albert Bridge Road, which ran alongside the park, and I tried to imagine what the people in the Road and the Drive were like. I thought of them, in layers of couples, sleeping peacefully side by side. The husbands might be tired out by do-it-yourself, having rawl-plugged themselves into a delicious stupor. The wives, having worried the last facts from *Family Doctor* and the *Nursery World*, might be lying awake thinking of their children and the sacrifices they would make for education.

The Road and the Drive, whatever else, were the local keeps of the professional classes, of people who were vigilant against any attempts to reduce the tone of the neighborhood. They had a formidable tenants' association. If they knew about the wife-swapping parties in nearby Sidney Court, they would form a vigilantes' committee for the belt overnight.

But there were also pockets of resistance in the Road and the Drive. There were odd corners where hospitality was all, where discussion was wild, where men who wore shiny shoes and matching socks were suspect. I wished that I'd known more about Battersea before I left.

On the road through the park, we passed some lonely single men and lonelier pairs of girls. I waited for a gap, then told Helen how well she was looking. After a long time, there is always the moment when you see your wife as a stranger might. Throughout our married life, I'd acknowledged men's remarks about my "beautiful wife" as if they'd said, "Fine day!" Now I was discovering that they hadn't been flanneling me.

"I wish I could say that you were looking well," she

said, "and it doesn't do drip-dry shirts any good when you wash them with soap and don't rinse them properly."

"Why didn't you answer my letter from Scotland?" I asked. "I thought you would answer that one."

"I was going to," she said, "then I got—well, not jealous . . . but angry. This line about loving Ruth Fleming, as if you were telling me something. And the slightly ungallant innuendo that *one* day, even *I* would be happy. I was going to answer it. I wrote three times and tore the letters up. I was going to answer, all right, then your other letter came."

The Big Dipper took its last dip of giggling girls and their high cries carried over the rattle of the exit turnstiles. A till keeper closed his sentry box, put to the painted gate and hurried off in a muddy hat and an anonymous rain-coat, head down against the wind; through the sauntering men in jeans and jackets, through the brave girls still in summer dresses.

"I'm sorry," Helen said. "That isn't a good enough excuse. I should have answered straightaway. But, even when I didn't want you, it wasn't easy to hand you over to Ruth Fleming. I can't quite explain that. Maybe it's the habit of being jealous which is difficult to lose. Poor Malcolm had it, too."

"Anyhow, that's over," I said.

"You think that, do you? I can't see you and Ruth staying apart for very long." Her laugh was forced. She said I had a rendezvous with Ruth at some disputed barricade.

Like sea horses in an aquarium, the funfair hobby horses still wheeled slowly, paint and surprise on their fishy faces. In front of us, a girl with a slim, beautiful body was play-fighting with a boy friend, on a cycle. With one foot on the pavement and one on the pedal of his cycle, he was

185

gliding—one foot in youth and one in manhood.

"You!" the girl said to the boy as they struggled.

"You!" the boy said to the girl.

Another young man cycled in circles, passing and re-passing the couple. Each time he reached them he said in an unnaturally deep voice, "Well. I don't know. I don't know."

"What don't you know about it?" the girl shouted at him in a suddenly nasal, angry voice.

I got Helen a cab and saw her off to where she was going. "Cheerio," I said.

"Cheerio and the best of luck," she said. "Honestly, the best of luck. I mean it."

The phone box was close. If I was going to grow up, I couldn't be afraid of loving Ruth.

"Are you there?" Ruth's mother asked. This was her usual calling-up signal.

"Yes," I said. After all this time, I had to choose a night when she was looking after Jill, when Ruth was out.

"Tom!" Ruth's mother said. "Isn't that *strange?* She had a feeling you would ring tonight and I told her not to be a silly girl. She left a message in case you phoned. She asked me to tell you that she'll be at King's Cross at 8:35 tomorrow morning."

The elation was very strong, like drink when you're not used to it. "Give my love to Jill," I said.

"Jill's with her," she said. "Honestly, it was like an evacuation. The guard's van must be *packed* with their clothes."

The only flowers Ruth had ever talked about were petunias. How the hell did you get petunias at King's Cross at 8:35 in the morning?

186

About the Author

Marshall Pugh was born in Dundee, Scotland, in 1925, and was educated there. Apart from his war service with the Black Watch, he has been in journalism all his life, and has been a general-features writer with the *Daily Mirror, Evening Standard* and *Daily Mail,* and a regular contributor to *Punch* for several years. He has written many articles for the leading British newspapers and periodicals, and two novels. Marshall Pugh is married and lives with his wife and daughter in London. *The Chancer* is his first novel to be published in this country.